THE SNATCH

Recent Titles by Gerald Hammond from Severn House

THE DIRTY DOLLAR
FINE TUNE
FLAMESCAPE
GRAIL FOR SALE
INTO THE BLUE
A RUNING JUMP

THE SNATCH

Gerald Hammond

This first world edition published in Great Britain 2003 by
SEVERN HOUSE PUBLISHERS LTD of
9–15 High Street, Sutton, Surrey SM1 1DF.
This first world edition published in the USA 2003 by
SEVERN HOUSE PUBLISHERS INC of
595 Madison Avenue, New York, N.Y. 10022.

British Library Cataloguing in Publication Data

Hammond, Gerald, 1926-
  The snatch
  1.   Kidnapping - Fiction
  2.   Robbery - Fiction
  3.   Detective and mystery stories
  I.   Title
  823.9'14 [F]

  ISBN 0-7278-5895-5

Typeset by Palimpsest Book Production Ltd.,
Polmont, Stirlingshire, Scotland.
Printed and bound in Great Britain by
MPG Books Ltd., Bodmin, Cornwall.

Chapter One

In one of the modest but expensive houses which fronted what was generally acknowledged to be the most desirable street in the town, Robin Dunwoodie was reading a lecture to his daughter. For the purpose, he had taken her into his study, a severe room relieved by a view over the adjoining golf course. The room was lined with heavy books and equipped with a computer and all the paraphernalia and toys of the modern businessman. She was offered a hard, upright visitor's chair, across the desk from the executive chair occupied by her father. The invitation, Alice suspected, was an ominous sign rather than a gesture of hospitality.

She was right. Mr Dunwoodie came to the point with unwonted speed. 'Why,' he demanded rhetorically, 'can't you be more like your brother?'

This was unfair. Ronald, Alice's brother, had qualified as a solicitor and was now living in his own flat and making good money as a partner in a local firm. These were the sole criteria known to his parents and judged by them. Alice knew that he was given to roisterous living, drinking more than was good for him, indulging in the smoking of illegal substances and sometimes dipping a toe into more dangerous waters. He had also suffered occasional infections of the kind to which those with overaffectionate natures are vulnerable.

1

But Alice would have had no intention of betraying her brother, even if there had been the least chance of such revelations being believed, and she nobly resisted the temptation to reply to her father's question by enquiring whether he wished her to grow a penis. Instead, she maintained the dignified silence which she knew would exasperate him.

Not expecting an answer, Mr Dunwoodie surged on. 'You seem to expect me to support you indefinitely while you laze around; and God alone knows what you get up to when you're out of our sight. Well, my patience is just about at an end. If you'd get yourself a proper job—'

The injustice of it was too much for Alice. She had never been quite sure what her father did for a living. He called himself a financial consultant, whatever that meant, and the signs were that he did very nicely at it, but she was prepared to bet that in the process he did not contribute very much to the sum of human happiness and well-being. She broke her silence. 'I've had jobs,' she said.

Mr Dunwoodie chose the less colloquial and more literal interpretation of her words. 'You've had about twenty jobs. And if one of them lasted for more than a fortnight, I don't remember it. Jim McLeod said that if you'd shown some reliability as a shelf-stacker he'd have promoted you quite soon.'

'To checkout operative. And I'd have stuck there for the next twenty years.'

'At least you'd have been bringing some money in and providing your own pocket money instead of draining it away. God knows we've wanted better for you, but you seem to have been careful not to qualify for anything. You got good Highers, or whatever they call them now, in almost everything I've ever heard of. We would cheerfully have stumped up to put you through university, or any

2

other course you fancied, if you'd showed the least inclination. But no. You'd rather laze around, sucking the public tit. If you had had the least talent for domesticity, I'd have been hoping that you'd make a career out of marriage – but not to any of the young tearaways we've ever seen you with.'

Mr Dunwoodie paused. He would not have been too dissatisfied to see his daughter cohabiting, if it would get her out of the house, out of sight and mind and out of his thinning hair, but he had more sense than to say so. 'You can't even cook.' This again was unfair. Alice had been well taught at school and when she had the house to herself she took pleasure in preparing cordon bleu meals for herself, but if she admitted to that area of expertise she would become the family skivvy for ever after. 'Look at Jim's daughter, Sarah. Going steady with a respectable young man . . .'

This was about the unkindest cut of all. Sarah McLeod was going steady, and more than steady, with several young men. Alice secretly admired her. She herself had somehow remained a virgin, although to let her parents be sure of it would have undermined her efforts to convince them that she was now an adult and an individual with her own independent aspirations, not one to be confined within the trammels of conventional bourgeois society.

She looked at her father and it was as if she had never seen him before. What funny things faces were, she thought. On a basic bone-structure were superimposed half-random and half-inherited shapes of flesh and gristle and skin, diverging very little from a common mould but adding up to expressions and casts of feature which were deeply meaningful. She had never before noticed that her father's eyebrows were shaggy or that his nose had a Roman arrogance and a bump in the middle. Most of his face was pale, the blotchy colour being confined to his cheeks and nose. His mouth, usually full-lipped, was set in a narrow line and his eyes seemed to be looking at her forehead. What, she wondered, had become of the father who had been her comforter and protector? She had been his princess. What, for that matter, had become of the little girl who had looked up to him as a god? She felt tears lapping at her lower lids.

Mr Dunwoodie looked past his daughter's dark curls to a watercolour of partridges bursting over a hedge. He knew that if he saw tears, he would falter. He was nearing the end of his peroration. '. . . think that we're some sort of idiots,' he said. (Alice just managed to stop herself from nodding.) 'Well, it can't go on any longer. From now on, for as long as you're under this roof, one of us will go with you each week when you collect your dole, or National Assistance, or benefit or whatever it's called, and we'll take charge of it and put it towards your share of the housekeeping; and we'll give you as much pocket money as we think you deserve. It won't be a lot, to judge by present performance. We'll pay for your clothes, but your mother will choose them and they'll be chosen to make you look as a daughter of ours should look, presentable, not like some scruffy sort of a tart.'

He stopped, horrified. His tongue had run away with him, driven on by the need to break through her impassive stare. Where was the darling child who had so delighted him only a few years earlier? And how had she turned into this sullen but alluring siren who must surely be the target for every seducer in the western hemisphere? What had happened to the good old days when a temptress could be shut up in a tower in a haunted forest, secure from all but the most princely suitors?

Alice had felt her skin prickle as the blood drained away. 'Finished?' she asked.

Her father felt anger rise again like bile. 'I think I've said enough,' he snapped.

'More than enough,' Alice said huskily. She jumped to her feet and left the room with as much dignity as she could muster. She wished that she had countered her father's words with a reasoned justification, analysing the stresses to which a young girl is subjected while on the threshold of adulthood. She could have pointed out that her usual dress of jeans and a jumper could hardly be considered tarty and that when she went out for the evening she was certainly not scruffy but dressed, as now, in exact conformity with the fashion among her peers. The reasoning had been there, intuitively rather than intellectually understood, but even if she had had the words they would have stuck in her throat. The habit of non-communication had become too deeply ingrained.

She paused in the hall and blinked back tears while she glanced at herself in the mirror. She definitely did not look like her idea of a tart. Sophisticated, rather. Her features were regular, her skin was good, her brown eyes lustrous and her lips full. Her dark hair had curled of its own accord and owed nothing to artifice. Her makeup was strong, but this was the fashion and her natural colour called for it. Her skirt was no shorter than the norm and if the material clung enough to show off a rather good figure . . . well, her parents had never objected to her being seen on the beach in a wet bikini. Her parents, her world, were so unfair.

Her mother came out of the kitchen – round-faced, slipping into plumpness, a motherly figure as mothers should be. Mrs Dunwoodie spent much of her time supporting Good Causes and had a part-time job with some charity shop. 'Going out, dear? Put your coat on. It's cold outside. Winter's coming.'

Alice was too fed up to make a civil answer. Anyway, her mother's four remarks had hardly been worth verbalizing. She was tempted to leave her coat behind as a gesture of defiance, but the wind was coming off the North Sea direct from Norway and it would indeed be cold outside. She grabbed it furiously off the hall-stand. This coat, at least, being quilted and coming down almost to her ankles, had been approved by her parents. She checked that her key was in her pocket and slammed out of the house. She considered herself a laid-back sort of person; she had always been slow to anger, but she was furious now. The injustice of it! She had gone for enough interviews for more challenging jobs. Her lack of formal qualifications had counted against her although her looks had been a greater drawback when interviewed by the sexless females who dominated personnel departments; but did she get any credit for her ambition? The fact that she had kept these aspirations secret from her parents was no excuse. They should have guessed. She was being childish, she knew, but they drove her to it.

The evening was cool even for late October and dry, but there was no moon and the trees in the landscaped front gardens shaded the path. She felt her way carefully to the front gate and stepped out onto the pavement. The trees which lined the street like sentinels had already been bronzed by the first frosts and they glowed brightly in the light of the street lamps. She decided to see who was in The Pantry. This was a recently opened bistro where coffee or wine by the glass or quite passable snacks were to be had. It was becoming popular with the younger crowd.

Her walk only took her to the end of the road, round

one corner and a hundred yards along a pavement beside a minor main road. The Pantry had been created in premises where a local shop had been driven out of business by the booming supermarkets; but the decor had been cleverly designed, combining the comfort of home with just a suggestion of jolly depravity. The younger crowd was attracted because it looked more expensive than, in fact, it was.

The younger crowd, however, had not yet arrived in strength. An elderly couple lingered over coffee in a corner and there was a young man with spots hunched over an evening paper, but Alice was relieved to see a fair-haired girl of about her own age at a table, communing with the smartly dressed waitress. Sarah McLeod, after a half-hearted stab at an accountancy degree course, had lowered her sights and pursued her further education as far as a secretarial and bookkeeping qualification and was now on the books of a secretarial agency as a 'temp' – which, she had told Alice, meant that she worked fewer weeks than a secretary in full-time employment but made about the same money. She was slightly smaller than Alice, slightly thinner and sometimes seemed slightly less intelligent, which made Sarah's modest success in the job market another example of the general unfairness of fate, but Alice had always managed to smother any feeling of envy and the two girls, who lived only a few doors apart, had remained firm friends through school and into adult life.

Their greeting, as usual, was encompassed in an exchange of smiles, backed up by a monosyllabic and unintelligible sound which might have been taken for 'Hey!' or 'Hi!'

Alice, mentally counting the coins in her purse, ordered a glass of red wine. 'You look fed up,' she said.

'That's putting it mildly,' Sarah said. 'My parents

have been going on at me to marry Gordon Watkins, just because he and my dad were once buddy-buddies. I don't suppose he wants to marry me any more than I want to marry him, but they won't listen. I'm not working just now and the house feels like Barlinnie.'

'Tell me about it!' Alice said. 'My father's just read me a lecture about buckling down and becoming a credit to the community and a prop and support to him in his old age, or something like that – I wasn't listening to all of it. But you could do worse than marry Gordon. At least he's rich.'

'There is that, I suppose. He seems to have blown most of what came to him from his father by now, but I think he still has one or two well-heeled uncles to go. It's a pity that I can't stand him. He used to be left in charge of me and you wouldn't believe what he got up to.' There was a break in the conversation as the waitress brought Alice's red wine and, for Sarah, a pink concoction with an umbrella on top. 'If it's any help,' Sarah resumed, 'and you want to throw a sop to your parents, my dad has an opening for a trainee bookkeeper. He said he'd be glad to have you back and if you cared to take the accountancy course you could work on up. You were always good at figures; and computers seemed to make sense to you.'

'Not really. Cyberprat dot com,' Alice said.

'Rubbish. I can only use them as sort of super-typewriters but you seem to think the same way they do.'

'I'll bear it in mind,' Alice said lightly. She was still furious, but the world began to look a little brighter. 'Jobs are a bore. I keep looking in the job centre in the hope that something might turn up that wouldn't be the yawn to end all yawns, maybe with a circus or something, or a professional hit-girl, but no such luck. If I took a job, any old job . . . Sarah, do you think we could get a small flat to share? That might make it worthwhile.'

'It's a thought,' Sarah said. Her babyish face took on an anxious expression. 'We could get out from under. But – don't be offended – you'd have to get a job that you could stick at. I wouldn't want you copping out and leaving me stuck with the rent and no company.'

'I could stick at digging ditches,' Alice said, 'if I never again had to listen to anybody asking me where I'd been and who I'd been with and why I was late home and when I was going to get a proper job.'

'I know the feeling,' Sarah said. 'Not in those exact words, but near enough.' They had finished their drinks. 'I've got a couple of new CDs, skate-punk, and my parents are out. Let's go and do some serious listening.'

Back in the cold night air, they walked briskly. A trio of boys whistled at them. Alice put her nose in the air but it was nice to be noticed. Almost opposite her parents' house there was a break in the regular, prosperous rhythm of the street at the large and overgrown garden of a big old house at present unoccupied. A slightly down-at-heels van had been backed into the driveway.

'One more fart out of you,' Tod Bracken said, 'and I'm going to give the girl up and go home.' He wound down the van window, pointedly.

'You haven't got a home,' Foxy Brett reminded him. His given name was Dougal but that was almost forgotten and he had become known as Foxy because of the various odours that followed him around. 'Maisie kicked you out,' he added.

'I'll get another home. I'd rather move in with Fat Brenda than choke in here. Just keep watching for a blonde girl, about nineteen or twenty. She usually comes

past here about now. And stick your arse out of the window.'

' "Keep a low profile," you said. People would remember.'

He had a point. 'All right. There's a piece of hose in the back,' said Tod. 'Put one end out of the window . . .' He began to explain in considerable detail what Foxy was to do with the other.

'There's two of them coming,' Foxy said suddenly. 'Is one of them the one we want?'

Tod wiped the misted windscreen and peered out. 'The blonde one.'

'So she's got company. It's off, then? Again?'

Tod roused himself. 'No. Damned if it is. We've buggered about long enough. The street's empty for once and here she comes. We'll take them both. Two for the price of one.'

Chapter Two

That part of Alice's mind which was not still seething at her father's words was toying more cheerfully with the delightful fantasy of escaping from home and setting up again in a flat with Sarah and possibly even with a job which was not too impossibly boring. The sudden appearance of two men to bundle them into the back of the van was so far outside her train of thought, and yet somehow not discordant with the mood of escape into a new and more exciting life, that the two girls were seated inside the van, breathless but otherwise unhurt, before she had absorbed what was happening. Even if a gruff voice, with more than a trace of a Glasgow accent, had not told them to be quiet on pain of unspecified sanctions, she never thought of screaming until it was much too late.

The van had evidently been used to transport building workers, because there was hard seating along both sides, a scattering of tools underfoot and a large box behind the front seats. Alice was elbow-to-elbow with Sarah. A large man had installed himself opposite and sat with one hand on the door handle, a small automatic pistol in the other. The doors closed and the other man climbed into the front. Alice had a glimpse of the interior while the flickering courtesy light was on.

The engine turned over sluggishly and then grumbled into life and the van moved off. It sounded as though it had already done enough work for one lifetime. The seats were smooth and there was no easy handhold available, so that at first the girls were preoccupied with not falling among the jumble of buckets and trowels on the floor. Alice found that her mouth was dry, there was a knot in her stomach and her mind seemed to have frozen. When girls were abducted, they were not always recovered alive.

When the van emerged onto the straight of the main road out of town and the yellow light of the street lamps began to flick by with the monotony of a lighthouse beam, Sarah found a high-pitched voice. 'What's the idea?'

'Shut up!' said the man opposite. 'Don't give me grief or you'll do the journey tied up and gagged. And you wouldn't like that. Or, I don't suppose you would.' In contrast to the harshness of his words and an accent which did not suggest a gentlemanly upbringing, his voice had a more kindly timbre.

The driver came to the first roundabout. The other man leaned forward to see past him. 'Left here,' he said, 'and then follow your nose. And for God's sake try not to gas us. There's two well-brought-up young ladies in here.'

'I can't help it,' said the man at the wheel. 'It's all that fibre.' His accent was similar but stronger, his voice more metallic.

'It's all that beer,' retorted the other.

Alice's mind began to work again. She sat in silence, weighing up their situation. This was not, as she had thought during the first, mad moment, a practical joke by two of their wilder friends. So whatever was in store for them did not bode well. On the other hand, the revelation of human frailty was somehow heartening. She pushed aside her fears and tried to tell herself that at least it was a break from the monotonous routine of friction at home and frustration outside it. Their captors might not mean well by them, but Alice had had enough of intimidation, even if of a less physical kind. She was not going to be dominated.

'If what you have in mind is a bit of rape—' she began.

'Good God, no!' In prison, Tod knew, sex offenders were near the bottom of the pecking order, with only child molesters below them. Despite coming from a social stratum in which almost anything went, it had been drummed into him by a whole gaggle of female relatives that the line between being masterful and actual rapine was never to be crossed. 'Nothing like that.'

'Oh!' Alice fell silent again. She set no great store by her virginity. Those of her friends who had discarded theirs seemed to be pleased rather than regretful over the loss, but after endless cautionary lectures from her mother she had never been certain that the pleasures or social advantages would be worth the one irreversible step. To lose it by coercion would be a return of humiliation and oppression in another form but at least it need leave no residue of guilt. She had hoped for an opportunity to insist that, if rape was intended, it should at least be safe rape. She had also intended to express a preference. The two men were not masked or disguised in any way – itself an ominous indicator – and fleeting glimpses had been enough to assure her that the man opposite her was distinctly the better looking of the two as well as being slightly better spoken. And she had already established that the other man offended in another way. Sarah would have been welcome to him.

But it seemed that no violation was intended. Tod's denial had been shocked enough to be sincere. So one possible avenue for winning over their captors seemed to be closed.

Sarah remained quiet but Alice could feel her trembling. 'Cheer up,' she said. 'At least it's a break in the monotony.'

'You be quiet,' Tod said firmly.

'Or you'll do what?'

'I'll think of something, believe me. Now shut up.'

'Say please.'

'Please,' Tod said before he could bite the word back. He silently cursed himself. Kidnap victims were supposed to do what they were told, weren't they?

Alice put a comforting arm round Sarah but she nodded to herself. After years of struggle for domination with her parents, she could recognize any sign of weakness. She looked out through the windscreen. They were rather off her beaten track but she recognized the ranks of tall beeches. She knew where they were.

After more than half an hour, they turned off a dual carriageway onto a network of minor roads and finally onto a farm track which had seen little use for some years. Outside the beam of the headlamps was blackness but Alice sensed that the countryside was open. The van bounced and groaned over potholes, and weeds scraped the underside. It brought them at last to a barn, derelict-looking in the light of the headlamps and half hidden by trees. Even with its big doors gaping, it looked uninviting.

Foxy drove inside, killed the van's engine and lights and got out to drag the barn doors closed. Tod fumbled a portable gas-lamp out of the box, lit it and stepped down to place it on the floor of the barn.

'You can come out now,' Tod said. 'Make yourselves at home.'

The two girls climbed down out of the van and looked

around. They were unimpressed with their surroundings. The earth floor was stained with pigeon droppings and cluttered with discarded sacks, an old harrow and, in one corner, a great heap of straw. In the upward light the two men looked tall and menacing, like devils attending to the furnaces of hell, but Alice found that fear was being swamped by a revival of anger. 'What the hell's this?' she asked.

'This is home for the next few days. Better make the best of it.'

'And just where are we supposed to sleep?'

'There are two sleeping bags in the box,' Tod said. He made his voice take-it-or-leave-it without, he hoped, any trace of apology. 'You can have those. Sleep in the van or –' he indicated the pile of straw – 'straw's warm and soft. Take your pick.'

Sarah was regaining confidence. 'And you'll be in the straw? It's not much of a choice. Where do we wash?' she asked.

'And pee?' said Alice. Tod hesitated. 'And I don't suppose you thought to bring any food,' she added.

'You're wrong there,' Tod said. 'Foxy, what food did you bring?'

For lack of anywhere to sit, they were standing around the gas-lamp in the middle of the floor-space, like guests at a cocktail party. The barn was cold and damp and it smelt musty. The wind came across the Scottish coast and the bare autumn fields and found the chinks in the boarding. Foxy gave up trying to close the last gap in the doors and came to join them. 'I got pork pies,' he said. 'Only three, but we can share them out. There's sandwiches – lettuce and ham. There's milk and teabags and a kettle and a gas ring in the van. And there's a canister of water. We should get by.'

'And for breakfast?' Alice said. 'No, don't tell me, I don't want to know.' The pistol in Tod's large hand, she now noticed, was identical to a cigarette lighter belonging to her father, so making a run for it should not present any immediate dangers. To gain a few instants, she drew in her breath, pointed dramatically into a corner of the barn and then ducked past Tod and sprinted out through the gap in the doors. No shot followed her, so it seemed that her guess had been good.

Her eyes had become accustomed to the bright gaslight and she ran into a world which was a sphere of black velvet with only a few pinpoints of light to help her tell up from down. It was a world with an uneven floor so that she staggered and stumbled and almost tripped. To judge by the sound of pursuit, only one man had come after her and he was having the same difficulty. She heard him swear as he tripped and nearly fell and she thought that she might be able to hide in the darkness, get to help, fetch the police to the barn in time to save Sarah. Then she ran full tilt into a wire fence and rebounded into the path of her pursuer. They met with an impact which knocked the breath out of her, but at least they were saved from a clash of heads by the fact that they were of different heights. That, she realized, meant that she was in the grip of the taller, non-smelly one.

Tod frog-marched her back to where the bright slit of light was escaping from the barn. Inside, Foxy had a grip on Sarah's arm but looked unsure what to do with it.

Tod gave Alice a push in the direction of Sarah and let her go. 'Don't you dare try that again,' he said gruffly, 'or we'll keep you locked in the van.'

Alice thought that being locked in the van might be preferable to life in the draughty barn, but she was in no mood to make what might be interpreted as concessions.

She squared up to him. 'I'm not making any promises,' she said. 'You've got to be out of your tiny minds if you think we're sleeping in mouldy straw and eating cold pork pie and supermarket sandwiches in a freezing barn.'

'See you, hen!' Foxy paused. The Glaswegian usually speaks surprisingly good English, heavily disguised by a strong accent and a layer of idiosyncratic slang. 'Who said you had to eat or sleep?' he asked indignantly. 'We're not going to no hotels. If you can do better, tell us about it.'

'I will,' Alice said. 'Let's get back in the van for the moment. At least there's somewhere to sit and the lamp may take the chill off.'

'I can't quarrel with that,' said Tod.

While Sarah was climbing into the van, Alice managed to catch Tod's eye. It was not a hostile eye and it looked rather sympathetic. She managed to indicate with her own eyes first Foxy and then the front of the van. Tod caught on quickly. He had no more desire than had Alice to have Foxy in their midst. 'Hop into the driver's seat,' he told the other man. 'We may have to run the engine to get the heater working.' Discarding tact, he added, 'And leave your window open a bit.'

Between the lamp and the residual warmth from the van's heater, the interior was soon comparatively snug. Tod filled the kettle and lit the gas ring. 'Now,' he said. 'You got some bright idea, let's hear it.'

'I know where there's a cottage,' Alice said. 'It's just as far from anywhere as this is, maybe further, and ten thousand times more comfortable. Some of my father's friends share a small fishing boat and they keep the cottage for sleeping in at weekends in summer.' In fact, the cottage belonged to Alice's father, but she had no intention of admitting her family's financial status until she saw how the land lay.

'We could go and look at it,' Foxy admitted.

'Why not?' Alice said. 'You've plenty of petrol.'

'How do you know that?' Foxy asked sharply.

'For Christ's sake,' Tod said, 'if I can see the fuel gauge from here, so can she.'

'Oh. Right.'

'Have you got any money?' Alice asked.

The cosy atmosphere chilled instantly. 'Why do you want to know that?' Tod demanded. 'We're out to get money, not to hand it over.'

'We're not going to live long on three pork pies,' Alice said patiently, 'and I don't suppose they left any food in the place when they shut it up for the winter. I think we pass a supermarket on the way there. If you don't have a credit card, let's have a kitty. I've got three quid.'

Sarah produced a five-pound note.

Male pride does not allow even a kidnapper to accept money from girls. 'Keep your money,' Tod said. 'We're not that broke. Write us out a shopping list.'

'Christ's sake,' Foxy exclaimed. 'What are you *doing*? This isn't how we planned it.'

'You got to be flexible,' Tod retorted. 'This could be better.'

'It could be a trap.'

'How the hell could it be a trap?' Tod sounded exasperated. 'They didn't know we were going to grab them. If there's any sign of people there, we turn round and come back here. What've we lost? No point suffering if we can be comfortable.'

'But a supermarket?'

'One of us can go in while the other stands guard.'

Between them, they found a pencil and a grubby sheet of paper. The kettle boiled. While the tea infused, Alice twisted round, rested the paper against the van's wall and, aided by Sarah, composed a shopping list. The tea, drunk from tin mugs, was surprisingly palatable. Sandwiches were produced. Sarah pointed out that they had already passed their sell-by dates but the girls were hungry and they shared one anyway. The men bolted the rest of the food.

The temporary amnesty seemed to be endangered when they parked in a remote corner of the supermarket car park. Under the van's feeble interior light, Tod scrutinized the shopping list. 'This looks a hell of a lot,' he said, 'Do you want to be comfortable or to live like pigs?'

'But I'll never find all this stuff. They don't put proper names on things any more.' Tod was beginning to sound plaintive. 'And I could write neater than that when I was five. How about you, Foxy? Could you pick out a whole lot of food in a supermarket?'

'God, no! I'd take all night and get the wrong things.'

Alice took back the list. She was recovering her spirits and with them the assumption of female superiority. 'Of course you would. I'll come in with you. Foxy – is that what you called him? – can stay here with my friend. It's all right,' she added quickly as she felt Sarah jump. 'I shan't run off and leave you to your fate.'

'You'd better not,' Foxy said, 'or she dies. Horribly. I got a knife.' He tried very hard to sound as though he meant it.

'Seems reasonable,' Tod said. 'Remember, I'll have the gun on you all the time. One false move and I'll shoot.'

'I bet you would, too. Well, are we going?'

Tod opened the back of the van and the two got out. Foxy took Tod's place and opened a large clasp knife. 'And no snatching a quick feel while we're away,' Alice said.

'Hey! I wouldn't do a thing like that,' Foxy said.

'I was speaking to my friend,' Alice said loftily.

Alice had been to the cottage several times in the past, but only as a passenger with no particular interest in the route. After several abortive casts, they resorted to a well-worn map and by a process of elimination found the correct track through farmland and then through a deep belt of forestry. Foxy was beginning to voice suspicions that they were being led a dance when they emerged unexpectedly from between the young conifers onto sandy ground with the smell and sound of the North Sea not far off in the darkness. The headlamps swung across a small building clad with cedar boarding. An overhead cable sprang out of the blackness to the top of a low gable. Beyond it, a sturdy workboat sat, supported by timber props, on a trolley evidently made from a lorry chassis. A startled fox bolted for the trees.

The hour was late. 'You're sure the place is empty?' Tod asked.

'Absolutely dead certain positive,' said Alice. 'You don't see any lights, do you? They hauled the boat out and shut the place up last month.'

'Let's get in, then,' Foxy said. 'I'm cold and tired and I'm hungry again and I want a pee. Bring the big screwdriver – we'll have to break in.' He stopped the engine and switched off the lights. The world went black.

'Keep the van's lights on for a minute. You won't need any screwdrivers,' Alice said. 'I know how to get in. Somebody bring the food carton.' She made a point of being first to the door and hid the digital lock with her body as she keyed numbers.

The door opened and she switched on a light. 'Electricity,' Tod remarked. He sounded impressed. Foxy killed the van's lights and came to join the party.

'That's what the overhead cable was for,' Alice said. 'But that's the only service that comes in. No phone. No mains drainage. Water comes out of a well and goes out into a soakaway, so think twice before you drink it unless it's boiled. And it has to be pumped up by hand, so don't waste it.'

They looked around. Alice's mother had given the place up as a bad job, so it had become very much a bachelor pad. Instead of pictures, the varnished pine walls had made it easy to provide nails and hooks and so were decorated with fishing tackle, boat gear, coils of rope and several charts. The main room was inescapably masculine but it was warm and comfortable and a palace compared to the barn. It was about the size of a three-car garage, but into it had been crammed two easy chairs, a rough dining table with ill-matched upright chairs and a kitchen fitment along one wall.

'It's quite warm,' Sarah said.

'They only leave the heating on low for frost protection,' Alice explained. 'It feels warm because we've just come in out of the cold. Bring your luggage in while I find all the switches and thermostats and things.'

'Luggage?' Foxy said. He was carrying a small haversack.

Alice sighed. 'Just sit down, then. I've only been here once before, but I think the bathroom's through there.'

Tod, exploring, found the bathroom and a small bedroom with a three-quarter bed. The former held a washbasin, a chemical toilet and, behind a plastic curtain, a primitive shower. A clanking sound and some overhead splashing suggested that water was being pumped into a cistern.

A rechargeable lantern sat on a shelf beside the door. Alice tried it and it lit brightly. 'I'm going outside for a few seconds,' she said.

The friendly atmosphere changed instantly to one of suspicion. 'You don't have to go outside to pee,' Tod said.

'I'm not going to pee. And I shan't run away.'

'I'll come with you and make damn sure of it.' Tod looked at Foxy, who held up the van's keys. Tod nodded.

Alice's errand took only a few moments. Her father, she knew, had dug over a small patch behind the cottage and planted a few vegetables. These had been consumed, but Alice knew that he had also planted some seeds which had grown into what amounted to a small hedge of parsley. She pulled a good handful.

The preparation of a meal was delayed because Sarah insisted on scouring each utensil before she would allow its use, but the cooking of a mixed grill was swiftly accomplished. The men waited, torn between renewed hunger and a desire to get down to business.

They squeezed themselves up to the table. Foxy took one look at the plate that Alice had put in front of him. 'What's all the green stuff?' he asked.

'Chopped parsley,' said Alice.

'I don't like parsley. You didn't put any on the others.'

'You're the one who needs parsley. For your flatulence.'

Tod looked up and emptied his mouth quickly. 'You mean it'll stop him farting?' he asked.

'I don't know that it'll stop him,' Alice said, 'but it'll make it smell less.'

'Does that really work?'

'It works with Labradors,' said Alice.

'Eat it,' Tod said.

The meal was eaten in an atmosphere which was almost companionable. When it was finished, Tod said, 'Now . . .'

'Not tonight,' Alice said firmly. She produced a huge yawn, not entirely feigned. 'It's too late and you're not going to do anything tonight anyway. We'll talk in the morning. We'll take the bedroom. There's an airbed and blankets and things in that cupboard in the corner.'

'Who says you're getting the bedroom?' Foxy asked.

Alice smiled. 'You two can have it if you like.'

'And have you run off? No way!' Tod said.

'Then we'll have it, which is what I said first time. You don't have to worry, you must have seen the bars on the windows. You two do the washing-up. And do it properly.'

As he plied the dish-towel Foxy said, 'How do those two get to order us around?'

'I don't know,' Tod said. He pulled an easy chair against the bedroom door. 'They just do it. There's going to be some changes in the morning.'

'We going to beat them up or something?' Foxy sounded both hopeful and awe-struck.

'Haven't decided. We've got to show them who's the boss. Anyway, you've got to admit that this is a bloody sight better than the barn. You can have the airbed tonight, we'll do a swap tomorrow.'

Nesting not uncomfortably together in the three-quarter bed which had once belonged in the Dunwoodie spare bedroom, the girls whispered far into the night.

Chapter Three

W ind, of the meteorological rather than the gastric kind, came with the morning. The cottage was partially sheltered by the trees a hundred and fifty metres away, but the girls woke to the sound of blown sand pattering on the roof. When Alice, carefully wrapped in her coat, pushed the bedroom door it was obstructed, but Tod pulled away the heavy armchair in which he had spent the night. Building workers are accustomed to early rising and the two men, if they had undressed at all, had dressed again in their working clothes and they were still dark with stubble.

'Thank you,' Alice said. Courtesy, after all, cost very little. 'Have you finished with the bathroom?'

'You can use it,' Tod said. He assumed his most threatening expression. His youth, spent in the shadow of an aunt, his mother and five sisters, was behind him but the habit of bowing to female authority remained ingrained; but surely, he told himself, he could order a couple of young female captives around. 'But first you've got to listen and no damn nonsense.'

One thing that the girls had agreed was that the initiative, and the dominant position, were not to be returned to the men. 'It can't be as urgent as all that,' Sarah said. 'We'll get washed and fix breakfast. After that, we'll talk all you want.'

The girls vanished into the bathroom and bolted the door, to manage as best they could with the kitchen soap. Foxy looked at Tod. 'I thought you said it was going to be different this morning.'

'I must have been joking,' Tod said. He forced his fists to unclench and breathed deeply. 'It *is* different. It's worse. Anyway, she's right about one thing. There's no hurry. Give the family time to get anxious.'

Alice and Sarah took their time with the electric shower. They returned to the bedroom and dressed as carefully as they could in the previous day's clothes. They came out at last. Tod was about to explode but Alice anticipated him. 'Breakfast first,' she said. 'Then we'll talk.'

Alice laid the table while Sarah began a fry-up. The men had done a creditable job of the washing-up and Alice was pleased to note that that the room was almost tidy and a window had been opened slightly for ventilation.

'I like cereal with my breakfast,' Foxy said plaintively.

'Not until your tummy's under control,' Sarah said. 'We couldn't put parsley on cereal.'

Tod decided to give affability a try. 'It wouldn't really go on bacon and eggs,' he said. 'Pity really. It worked a treat.'

Breakfast was disposed of in an appreciative silence. Alice cleared the debris away.

Tod slapped a writing pad down on the table in front of Sarah and put a ballpoint pen beside it. He resumed his ferocious scowl. 'You're going to write a letter to your parents. You're being well looked after for the moment but we want ten thousand pounds or else.'

'Or else what?' Alice asked.

'Let's hope that you never find out,' Tod said grimly.

'Well, I'm not going to write that we're being well

looked after,' Sarah said, 'because so far we've been looking after you.'

'You'll do as you're bloody well told,' Tod said. His voice had gone up. He dragged it down. 'You're in no position to argue.' He pulled the cigarette-lighter-pistol out of his pocket.

'Smoke if you want to,' Sarah said.

Tod pretended not to understand. 'You'll be sorry.'

Alice sighed. 'You haven't done your homework properly. I used to be made to stand in the corner for that. You're barking away up the wrong tree. Neither of our families has enough money to be worth risking jail for.'

There was a silence while the men evaluated that statement. 'You came out of a big enough house,' Foxy said at last to Alice. 'And what about your friend? Her father's Mr McLeod of McLeod's supermarket.'

The girls exchanged a covert glance. They had settled on their stories during the night. 'I'm the housekeeper's daughter,' Alice said.

'My dad doesn't own the supermarket,' Sarah chimed in. 'He's the manager. The name's a coincidence. He has a few shares in it – that was part of the deal when he took the job – but that's all. And it's barely making money at the moment since that big Fineway supermarket opened, half a mile up the road. They can barely compete. They have to keep lowering their prices, just to keep a share of the customers, and then Fineway just lower theirs even further. Dad's shares are worth about three-quarters of damn-all. He's been talking about chucking it up and going to work for Fineway. How much were you going to ask for me?'

'Like I said, ten grand,' said Tod. 'Worth it, aren't you?'

'Oh, I'm worth it,' Sarah said. 'I'm worth a fortune, but

that's just my opinion. My dad couldn't raise anything like ten grand, not without getting into hock for years. A sum like that would be enough to push him into going to the police, no matter what threats you made. And then you'd be in for the full treatment. A bag of dummy money with a homer in it, probably, and with invisible dyes and all the tricks in the book. They'd have you before you'd turned round.'

'And the courts don't like kidnappers, because awful threats have been made against the victims and it's no good saying later that you didn't really mean it,' Alice said. 'You're not very good at this, are you? You didn't check up on your facts or make proper preparations and you even let us see your faces. Were you planning to kill us later?'

'Not if they paid up,' said Foxy. 'We decided that you seeing our faces didn't matter. We don't come from around here.' He looked from one girl to the other through narrowed eyes. 'How come you didn't say any of this last night?'

'Two reasons,' Alice said. 'Firstly, you never said that it was ransom you were after. Secondly, we wanted to let you show your hand. We may have a use for you.'

'Like what?' Tod asked.

'We'll tell you once we're sure you're up to it. You haven't been very impressive so far, letting us see your faces.'

'It was going to be a one-shot thing,' Foxy said. 'See, we got a problem. We just wanted enough to get abroad, Spain or somewhere.' He looked from one to the other with spaniel's eyes. 'Help us, just a little bit, and we'll let you go.'

Alice laughed. 'Let us go? When we were in the supermarket yesterday, I had half a mind to whack Tod with a frozen turkey and call a security guard to fetch you out of the van. The question is rather, are we going to let you go?'

'You what?' said Tod.

Alice looked him in the eye. It was now or never. 'Sarah and I have our own ambitions. We want to get away together and have a place of our own, a life of our own. We just need a little money to get started. So you and we just possibly could be useful to each other. But, so that we know what we're getting into, what's this problem that you've got? Are you wanted for something really serious?'

The two men looked at each other. Tod shrugged. 'May as well tell you. There's nothing secret about it and nothing worse than a little fiddling. We're building workers, see? I'm a mason and Foxy's a digger-driver. We've been mates a long time. We came here to work on the new leisure-complex contract. First day here, we met a couple of birds.' He looked doubtfully at the two girls.

'It's all right,' Sarah said. 'We do know the facts of life.'

'I bet you do. Well, we moved in with them. It seemed a good idea at the time but we'd have been a hell of a lot cheaper in digs.'

'That's for sure,' said Foxy. 'We'd have been cheaper in a suite at the Ritz.'

'So they cleaned you out,' Alice said. 'That still doesn't make a problem. It's all right,' she added when both men hesitated, 'you haven't done anything wrong yet, except for hustling us into your van, and we won't make a fuss about that. You may as well tell us.'

'We still had our jobs,' Foxy said, 'but we were broke. So we signed on.'

'For the dole?' Sarah asked.

28

'They don't call it that now, but that's what it is. And we were caught out. The real trouble was, we'd done it before. They stopped our payments straight away and there's to be a prosecution if they can find us again. And, with people coming round and asking questions about us, we got laid off.'

'All we wanted from you,' Tod said plaintively, 'was a stake. Go somewhere abroad, Spain maybe, until it blows over.'

The conversation died. The two men looked miserably at each other. 'Couldn't we just stay here for a bit?' Foxy asked suddenly. 'We could get casual work and pay off what we were overpaid?'

Tod shook his head violently. 'We'd be right back where we were except for not having to sleep in the van.'

This was not in the plan at all. 'Not a hope,' said Alice briskly. 'There could be somebody out here any time, to fetch something or to read the meter. You could be had for breaking and entering if we weren't with you. Right. We'll take a break for thinking. While we do, let's get the place cleaned up. We'll do the kitchen bit if you sweep and tidy the rest.'

Obediently, the two men started on a rough and ready tour of the cottage. While the girls washed the dishes and restored the catering corner to their own standard of cleanliness, they returned to their whispered discussion. The men also were conversing sotto voce, but whereas the girls' whispers were punctuated by subdued giggles the men's debate bordered on argument and recrimination.

The girls washed the dish-towels and braved the wind to hang them to dry on an outside line behind the cottage. The wind had eased a little but it still took all the pegs that they could find to anchor the two towels securely to the line. In midmorning, Alice called a halt. If they had to evacuate the cottage in a hurry, it was unlikely that her father, who was not a pernickety housekeeper and was disinclined to scrutinize such things as electricity accounts, would notice that it had ever been occupied.

They put coffee on the table and a meeting was convened. Somehow it was tacitly accepted that Alice was in the chair. 'Right,' she said. 'Here's how we see it. You two need money to get out of the country. It seems to me that you might be better off asking whether the National Assistance Office, or whatever they call themselves now, would accept reimbursement of the money you fiddled by taking a proportion of what you can earn and drop the prosecution, but that's your business. Sarah and I are both putting up with repressive lives at home and we want to get out and share a flat.'

'Not lezzies, are you?' Foxy asked.

'No, we are not,' Alice said firmly. She decided to avoid mention of her own lack of sexual experience. 'We're definitely hetero but, just so that there are no misunderstandings, our taste does not run towards working men who are damn nearly old enough to be our fathers. Even a rented flat, if we could find one, would take money to furnish and we've hardly a bean between us; and we'd still have to find the rent. To cut a long story short, we could do with a substantial windfall, the same as you.

'So we're game to put a foot outside the law, but only if it's properly planned. I've read a lot about criminal cases and my . . .' She paused. She had nearly referred to her parents, but she had no wish to allow any thoughts of ransom to be resurrected. 'My mother's boss and his son are both lawyers although the boss has given it up and he acts as a financial consultant these days. I do know this much. Most criminals are caught because they get lazy and take short cuts. They don't plan for every contingency and they don't do everything that's possible to cover their tracks. Or they repeat themselves. Or they go after something so big that the truth's bound to come out. Or they get violent, so that all the resources of the law are turned against them. If we go ahead, we don't make any of those mistakes. Agreed?'

The two men nodded, mesmerized.

'This is going to take time and thought,' Alice said. 'We can stay comfortable here for long enough while we plan and prepare for one good score, but we need things. This is Thursday, isn't it?' More nods. 'Where I live will be empty all afternoon. Yours too?' she asked Sarah.

'Always,' Sarah said.

'Then we must pay a visit. Whose van is that outside? Stolen?'

'It's mine,' Foxy said.

'With the original number plates?'

'Yes.'

'And you were using it for a kidnapping? Compared to us, you're the original Babes in the Wood. While we're out and about, get some black paint and some white. It can go two-tone for a while and be changed back again quickly.'

'I'll choose my own colours, thank you,' Foxy said indignantly.

'You do that. First, go and clean it out. It's like travelling in the back of a bin-lorry.'

The van was butting into a stiff wind as it made its way back along the dual carriageway. 'But what are we going to do?' Foxy said. He had to raise his voice and turn his head to be heard above the struggling engine and the sound of the wind over the uneven bodywork.

'What is this clever caper that can't land us in the shit?'

'We don't know yet,' Alice explained patiently. 'We'll think of something. The world is full of places where money accumulates and people get careless after a bit, especially when it isn't their own money. We know that crooks do get away with things if they're careful enough. Only about a third of crimes are ever solved, so if we only sin once the odds are in our favour. Just keep thinking and watching and what we want will jump up and down in front of us, begging for attention. I'll tell you what it won't be. It won't be anything involving violence or ripping off some poor old soul. It won't be embezzlement, because we aren't in that sort of scene and anyway they usually get caught.'

'What about some sort of email fraud?' Sarah asked. 'That would be the easiest of the lot and you're a whiz on the Internet.'

'I'm not as good as all that. I might manage the first steps and it's possible to use the Internet and cover your tracks, but how you get your hands on any actual money without being traceable beats me. You can get somebody's credit-card number, but unless you have the actual card it seems to limit you to ordering things to be sent to you and selling them again. No, thank you very much. Takes too long and leaves too much of a trail and we just don't have the skills. Unless one of you happens to be a computer-literate hacker?'

'If we were,' Tod said gloomily, 'we wouldn't be knocking our pans on building sites, laying Irish confetti.'

'Laying what?' Alice asked.

'Bricks. What you said, you ruled out just about everything.'

'Not everything,' Alice said. 'Keep thinking.'

The van halted outside Alice's home. 'This isn't just a ploy to get away from us? No, I guess not,' Tod said quickly.

The van moved on towards Sarah's house.

Alice let herself in. Suzy, the family Labrador, greeted her enthusiastically, carrying her bowl and assuring Alice that nobody had fed her for days and she was starving to death. Alice had had the house to herself on most days but now, for some reason, she felt like a burglar. She found herself walking softly as she packed a selection of clothes into a duffel bag borrowed from the attic. She added a supply of toiletries and household sundries because, after all, if she had not been going away she would certainly have used her share of them. Then she sat down at the dining-room table with the laptop computer which had been her present on her recent birthday.

Dear Mum and Dad,

All right, so we've been getting on each other's nerves a bit. My fault, I suppose. I couldn't help being a teenager but that won't last for much more than another few months. Time is on my side.

I'm going away. To redeem myself, you might say. Don't worry about me, I'm not going on the streets. I'm going to get back on what you called a 'proper footing' and when I've done that I'll be back, not to stay but to visit. Please believe that I love you both very much, I'm just not very good at showing it.

Enjoy the peace and quiet. Love, Alice.

She printed the letter and signed it. She considered adding a kiss at the end but decided not to go over the top.

She left it in a conspicuous position on the kitchen table, then stowed the computer and printer carefully in the bag, well padded with clothes, added the two battery-chargers and pocketed her mobile phone. She visited her father's study for one more item.

A last look around and she seemed to have everything. But she would be coming back. Or, apart from one hasty visit, was this a final farewell? She felt hollow inside, like her first day at school. She was preparing to step over that line which must not be crossed. But, she told herself, she would be very, very careful. And, if the worst came to the worst, could her parents be any more disapproving than they were at present? A suitably contrite attitude would be such a welcome change that they would surely come around.

Rather than keep the van waiting and attracting the attention of the Neighbourhood Watch, she carried the heavy bag outside. Suzy was determined to join her for a good walk but was firmly left behind. Alice had taken her time but there was no sign of the van. Sarah must be emptying her house.

'Hello, Alice dear,' said a voice. Alice jumped. Screened as she was from the road, she was sure that she was alone. But a head had appeared over the garden wall, a round face with a toothy smile, crowned with tight silver curls. Alice cursed her luck. Mrs Dundee was a nosy neighbour but she was usually at bridge on a Thursday afternoon. 'Going away?'

Alice muttered something about 'a bit of a holiday'.

'How lovely! Somewhere nice and warm?'

Alice was tempted to place herself in Australia, but that would be too easily contradicted later. 'Not very far,' she said. 'I'm going to stay with a friend.' That, at least, was more or less true. She could see that Mrs Dundee was about to start an inquisition. The lady might be curious but she was easily diverted. 'No bridge today?'

The diversion was a success. Mrs Dundee launched into an explanation involving the illness of one member of the usual four, including details of every symptom and a summary of diagnoses both false and correct. She was going on to summarize the efforts which had been made to find a replacement when Alice heard the van's engine, further along the road, struggle to respond to the starter. 'Got to go,' she said quickly, 'or I'll miss my lift. I hope your friend's better by next week. I may be coming back to take a phone call but after that I'll be gone for a while.'

With that uninformative remark, she hurried out of the gate and along the pavement. She caught the van as Foxy was making a six-point turn. Mrs Dundee was hidden by trees, and, although Alice had sometimes suspected the lady of having X-ray vision and telescopic eyes, it might not be a disaster if she was seen getting into a white van. Just something else for her parents to worry about. She heaved her bag into the back of the van and climbed in after it. Most of the floor-space was taken up by Sarah's two suitcases.

At the end of the road Foxy glanced over his shoulder. 'Where to now?'

Alice had been thinking. 'Head for the Fineway super-market. We won't live very long on what we bought yesterday. We need all sorts of supplies.'

'We don't have any money,' Tod groaned. 'You cleaned us out.'

'Leave the thinking to me,' Alice said. 'I've borrowed my . . . my mum's employer's credit card. His wife does all the shopping on her card and fills up the car and all he ever does is pay the account without even looking at it. As long as we put the card back within about the next two hours, nobody's going to notice.'

'What about the signature?'

'I can manage.' Alice had been copying her father's signature for years on her school reports. It was just good luck that he had a unisex first name.

There was a heavy shower, rain bouncing off the tarmac. The van's wipers were hard put to it to cope. They trundled down a road lined with service industries and blocks of low-rise flats and passed the local police headquarters of the county constabulary. The town was neither large enough nor rough enough to require a force of its own. A bridge carried them over the river. All summer the river had been bustling with boats but these had been pulled out for the winter and were ranked along the broad roads flanking the riverside. The empty water was matt with the rain.

Beyond the bridge, they were in the town centre. The pleasing mixture of old and new was marred by a large site, usually noisy with machines, where the new leisure complex was beginning to rise above ground. Further on they passed a row of shops which had once served the daily needs of the community but now, forced to diversify, were mostly given over to estate agents and building societies.

The Fineway supermarket loomed beyond. Blank-faced except for the acreage of automatic glass doors, it could have been mistaken for a cinema complex. Opposite, there was a modern Clydesdale bank, looking flimsy compared to the older structures around it. The car park at the side of the supermarket was mostly filled, except for the spaces reserved for handicapped drivers which were noticeably empty, but there was ample space in the larger car park behind the building. Small trees were spaced regularly around the perimeter. Nature in a straitjacket, Alice thought.

The rain had stopped and the tarmac was draining slowly. Foxy parked facing the back of the supermarket, a large blank wall pierced only by a small door where a woman in an overall was enjoying a surreptitious smoke. He carefully avoided parking among the puddles. 'What about that bank across the road?' he suggested.

'We are definitely not bank robbers,' Alice said severely.

'I was thinking of the cash machine,' Foxy said. 'I've heard of them being fetched out by a good pull by a vehicle.'

'If it's been done,' said Sarah, 'I bet they'll have fixed them in more solidly by now.'

'No harm looking,' said Alice. 'While we shop, you two blokes take a look, one at a time. Don't go in or loiter, just walk past and think about the questions we'd want answered. Would your van pull it out, do you think? Is it overlooked by security cameras? If the answers are yes and no, one of us will go in tomorrow and ask questions about opening an account and take a look from the inside.'

'That sounds like sense,' said Tod. 'You got a head on your shoulders.'

The girls were back at the van in just under an hour, wheeling two trolleys laden with cartons. The men, it had transpired, had lost all their personal possessions when relationships with their lady-friends deteriorated into warfare. Since then, they had been living rough in the back of the van – which, Sarah said, explained a certain lack of personal freshness. Soap powder, toothbrushes and razors were displayed on top of one of the cartons and the other revealed two cheap towelling bathrobes. Foxy got out to help them load up. 'You were a hell of a time,' he said.

'We went round at breakneck speed but we had to get a hell of a lot of food,' Alice retorted. 'We may not be able to do this again. And there were other things. Turn right outside the car park and left at the end. You're going to need fuel.'

Foxy complied. As he drove, he said, 'They've redesigned those cash machines. There's damn-all to get hold of. The slots are so narrow that any hook you could put in would break or straighten out before it shifted the casing. And there's security cameras all over the place. How about here?'

'Drive on.' They rolled past a large and garish filling station. 'We want somewhere I've never been before and where there aren't any cameras,' Alice said. 'But not too small or they won't keep aerosols of paint. You can pay cash for the paint, we don't want it showing up on the credit-card slip.'

'No money,' Tod said. 'You cleaned us out last night. I told you, but you can't have been listening.'

Alice was tired. 'I was listening,' she snapped. 'Leave the thinking to us, you aren't very good at it. I can give you money.' Alice had accepted a substantial sum as cashback from the supermarket. 'Get enough black paint, or whatever colour you fancy, to do the bottom half of the van and enough white to change it back again in a hurry.'

On the outskirts of the town they found a filling station which passed all Alice's criteria and they bought paint and filled the van to the filler-cap with fuel. As they passed Alice's home, there was no sign of her parents' return and Mrs Dundee seemed to have been driven indoors by the rain. Alice had Foxy drive on to the end of the road. She walked back and returned the credit card to its usual hiding place. She kept her key. Suzy looked at her reproachfully.

'Home, James,' she told Foxy.

It was late afternoon when they arrived back at the cottage. They were hardly in at the door before Foxy started raking through the cartons. 'What's for supper?'

For the moment, Alice was only interested in sitting down. Pavements and supermarket floors were hard on feet which were wearing thin shoes, and the seats in the back of the van were hardly restful. The front passenger's seat had a loose spring which was apt to trap the unwary. 'You'll see all in good time,' she said. 'First, you two go and shower and shave and put on these robes while we give your clothes a wash. Lord!' she added. 'I'm beginning to sound like my mother.'

Tod was close to the point of explosion. Alice's remark about thinking had rankled. Sarah hastened to calm the atmosphere. 'We're going to need you at least halfway respectable,' she explained. 'We thought of buying you some new clothes, except that we don't know yet what parts we may want you to play.'

'We're not actors,' Tod said.

'Maybe not,' said Alice. 'But if you try to do *anything* looking like you are now, the police will be all round you before you've stepped over the threshold. We can always dirty you up again if whatever we decide to go for needs a couple of tramps or real toughs. Chuck your clothes out, and shower before you put on the robes. We may need to wear them.'

'I don't know about your mother,' Foxy said, 'but you sound exactly like mine. Look like her, too.'

Tod was already heading for the bathroom. 'He's

paying you a compliment,' he said over his shoulder. 'His mum's a real looker. I quite fancy her.'

'His dad must have been hideous,' Sarah said.

'We've never been quite sure,' said Foxy, quite unperturbed. 'My mum said that one of the possibles was no' bad looking.'

Chapter Four

The evening was well advanced before a meal of lamb chops with three vegetables was on the table. The day had cleared and there was a fresh, dry wind in which the hand-laundered clothes were billowing satisfactorily. The two men were sitting in wait, shaved, clean and wrapped in the towelling bathrobes. They looked unfamiliar and strangely vulnerable. Tod was now seen to have a firm but cleft chin which completed his well-assorted features, producing a face which, if not handsome, was regular and imbued with enough character to be pleasing, even if that character spoke of a placid mildness rather than the assertiveness which grime and stubble had suggested. And, Alice noticed suddenly, he had *dimples*, for God's sake! Foxy, while looking ten times less disreputable than previously, still had the sharp features of one who would not hesitate before lifting a charity box from a pub, but at least he carried a greater personal freshness with him.

They had made do with the last of Foxy's sandwiches for lunch and the men had had no time for snacks in between, so there was silence except for appreciative noises while the main course was enjoyed. Tod was moist-eyed with pleasure. The sole complaint came from Foxy, who was indignant at the lack of beer, but he was out-voted. With fruit, cheese and mugs of tea to finish with, talk became possible.

41

'So far,' Alice said, 'I've had plenty of thoughts but none that doesn't have some serious snag. We're trying to think of something non-violent. Doesn't any one of us know enough about computers to hack into a bank, move money from one account to another and obliterate the transaction?' She received three negative looks with head-shakes and smiled ruefully. 'A pity! That would have been ideal. Perhaps we should study it up. I'm sure there are books, or somebody must run a course. Otherwise, it seems to me that we need a place where money collects in the form of cash.'

'I thought you said that violence was out,' Tod said.

'It is. I wasn't thinking of holding up a filling station. I was thinking more of somewhere that money lies over-night. Has anyone any bright ideas?'

Into an anxious silence, Sarah dropped the word 'Black-mail.'

The silence returned for a shocked few seconds. The word had unpleasant connotations, but there was no doubt that it fell within Alice's parameters. 'But we don't know anybody's guilty secret,' Alice said.

'I do,' said Sarah smugly.

Alice's first thought was that Sarah should have kept her ideas to herself until they were alone rather than commit them to sharing with the men whose partici-pation seemed unnecessary. Her second was that Tod and Foxy could make any overt contact with the vic-tim and carry the onus if by any chance something should go seriously wrong. The ethics of it seemed to be irrelevant. If somebody had behaved badly enough to be open to blackmail and carelessly enough to be found out, they deserved to pay for their sins; and a cash payment now would be better all round than landing the taxpayer with the cost of prosecution and possibly incarceration. 'Who do you have in mind?' she asked cautiously.

'Gordon Watkins.'

Alice's faint recollection of Gordon Watkins was of a person not well endowed with charm, but there was one snag to the otherwise sound proposal. 'You won't be able to marry him if you rip him off. That's if he has to know that the idea came from you.'

'That's another advantage. I wouldn't marry him if he came two-for-the-price-of-one and with trading stamps. When I was eleven or twelve and he was about sixteen, whenever my parents wanted to go out for the evening they used to get him in and leave him in charge. He used to go as minder to several other houses and I know three other girls . . .'

'He abused you?' Tod asked in a hushed voice, scandalized.

Sarah shrugged. 'I suppose you could call it that. I didn't mind a lot at the time. To be honest, I thought it was all rather funny. He was so repressed that it's a wonder he ever managed to come even that far out of his shell. He was more interested in my undies than in me. And he liked to be tied up.'

Foxy sniggered.

'He'd certainly pay up to keep that out court and of the papers,' Tod said. 'But what sort of money does he have? How much could we ask before he decided that he'd rather face the fuzz and the publicity than pay up?'

'There's the rub,' said Sarah. 'He had a good legacy from his father a few years ago, so he moved out into his own flat and started living it up. His mother was saying that he pulled his horns in recently. She thought that he had matured at last, but my guess is that he was running a bit short. He spent a bomb on his car but it's been in an accident, so he wouldn't get much for it now. I don't know how far he could be pushed, but it wouldn't be a lot, shared round four of us.'

'What's his job?' Tod asked.

'He's a surveyor. He works for that big building contractor who does just about everything around here. McTaggart and Campbell.'

'That's who we were working for,' Tod said. 'On the leisure centre. That's the only big contract they have just now. Would I have seen him around?'

'You might. He's thin and nervous-looking with black hair and slightly prominent front teeth which give him the look of a rabbit. And a sticking-out Adam's apple.'

Tod nodded. 'I know him. The bosses love him because he's good at the job, which mostly consists of cooking the measurements and looking for loopholes to claim extras under the contract, but the site staff take the piss out of him something wicked. He lost his rag once, which only made it worse. I thought he was going to cry.'

'That sounds like my boy,' Sarah said.

'Do they leave the wage packets in a site hut overnight?' Alice asked.

Tod laughed. 'God, no! Two men draw the money from the bank, cross the road, make up the packets and dish them straight out. Don't bother to say it again,' he told Alice. 'No violence and no armed robbery.'

'I wasn't going to,' Alice said coldly. 'Sarah, you've produced the only idea so far. Any other inspirations?'

'Only one,' said Sarah. She closed her eyes until Alice thought that she had fallen asleep and prepared to give her a shake. Sarah's eyes snapped open suddenly. 'But I don't think it would work,' she said.

'Tell us anyway.'

'Well, all right. It's the Fineway supermarket, the one

we were at this afternoon. I worked there during the summer after we left school, before my degree course started at the Commercial College – the one I flunked out of before I switched to the secretarial course, to save you reminding me,' she added in an aside to Alice. 'I was on the checkouts. I packed it in when Mr Farquhar, the manager, started calling me into the storeroom and trying to feel me up. They take in a lot of money.'

'I bet you some security firm comes in to collect it every few hours,' Foxy said. 'Men with helmets and baseball bats.'

'Not always,' Sarah said. 'That's the point. During the week, yes, it's just like you said. The pattern was always different on a Saturday. There was a boy there, a management trainee, who used to take me out for a coffee. He told me that the arrangement dated from when the supermarket was much smaller. If you look at the building, you can see that it's been extended twice. The security firm they used, and still use, charges much more for visiting after lunchtime on a Saturday, so the money stays in a safe in the manager's office overnight and all through Sunday until Monday morning. I suppose it's a system that's always worked so far, and their insurers have never thought to object, so they've never got around to changing it.'

'And they stay open all day Sunday,' Tod said thoughtfully. 'There must be all the money in the world in there by Sunday night. They have an off-licence and the only lottery machine for a long way round about.'

'It's probably mostly cheques and credit-card slips,' Foxy said.

'Some,' Sarah admitted. 'But it's amazing how many people pay in cash – especially in the off-licence, when they don't want the family to see how much they're

45

spending on booze. That's all very well, but I don't see how we could do it. It's a damn great safe in the manager's office and I think it's cased in concrete or something. I walked past the door when they interviewed me for the job. And there's some sort of electronic alarm in the room. It had a little red light that winked on for a few seconds every time I moved. It's probably connected to the police station after the supermarket closes.'

The silence returned, but dispirited. Hope had arisen and died.

Tod stirred. 'Where's the manager's office, then?' he asked.

'Right at the back,' Sarah said. 'Beside the door where we parked the van. Why?'

'Let's not give up just yet. Could we get a look at the plans of the building?'

'We could try the Planning Department,' Sarah suggested.

Tod shook his head emphatically. 'Planning drawings wouldn't tell us what we need to know. And they wouldn't let us look at applications made under the Building Regs. Let's think.'

'McTaggart and Campbell built the supermarket,' said Foxy. 'A contractor's supposed to return or destroy all drawings, but often it doesn't happen if they do all the alterations and maintenance. Did you say your boyfriend worked for them?'

'Is it important?' Sarah asked. 'I wouldn't want to waste good leverage over nothing. And may I remind you that he is my boyfriend the same way you and Tod are sisters? In fact, not by the remotest imagination.'

Tod pursed his lips. 'No promises. But it could be important. Let's think about it. While you two were farting about inside the supermarket, I had nothing to look at except the back wall of it. I noticed the pattern as it dried after that rain. You could see where there were concrete columns. That tells me that between the columns is infilled with something lighter, maybe brickwork.'

'Irish confetti?' said Alice. The phrase had stuck in her mind. She had once been invited to an Irish wedding.

'If you like. I could certainly reduce it to confetti. I could cut my way through that in minutes.'

'Would my van take the weight of a large safe?' Foxy asked. 'If it would, we could borrow a digger off the building site, load the safe into the van and cut it open in our own time.'

'Hold your horses,' said Tod. 'Don't breenge. When Sarah was telling us, it sounded as if the safe was backed against the outside wall but embedded in concrete. If that's right and if the concrete doesn't go down the back and if an infrared sensor from the front is all that's protecting it, we could cut straight through the wall and the back of the safe from outside the building.'

'If, if, if,' said Foxy. 'It's all bloody ifs.'

'What the hell did you expect?' Sarah demanded. 'A door left open for you and nobody looking? If I thought it was going to be that easy I'd have done it myself.'

'Cool it. This is the only possibly good idea we've had so far,' Alice said. 'So let's not squabble. Let's solve the problems one at a time and if we come up against one that we can't solve we'll drop it and look for something else. I suggest that Sarah phones her non-friend Gordon from my mobile this evening and reminds him that she knows things that he wouldn't want the world to know.'

'She mustn't say too much on the phone,' Tod said. 'You don't know who's listening. Or recording.'

'Absolutely right,' Alice said. 'I think we have to meet him very soon – but not tonight, it's getting too late for that. Tomorrow evening, then. We'll script what she has to say.'

While Sarah got up to find a paper and pencil, Foxy said, 'That gives us at least a day with bugger-all to do. Is it time to make my van two-tone?'

'Not yet,' Tod said. 'Not until we're ready to go outside the law. Right?' He looked at Alice. The habit of deferring to her was becoming entrenched.

Alice was not going to let her troops get slack. 'That's right,' she said. 'Give the inside of it a damn good scrub instead and do something about the loose spring in the passenger's seat. And we could do some more housekeeping and laundry in here. We need fresh milk and eggs and things, so, if we're going in to the town, one of us might try to get a look at the inside of the manager's office.'

The atmosphere became more cheerful. At least they were no longer stagnating but moving in what might or might not prove to be the right direction.

Sarah had to get the number from Directory Enquiries. Then there was no answer to the first call. It was almost eleven before the phone at the other end was lifted. 'Hello,' said a cautious voice.

'Is that Gordon Watkins?'

'Speaking. Who's that?'

Sarah looked down at the page of notes. 'This is Sarah McLeod. Are you alone?'

'Yes. Why?'

'You remember the fun and games you used to put me through? And Jenny McRobb and Moira James?'

There was a long pause. The voice, when it came again, sounded choked. 'I don't know what you're getting at.'

'I think you remember. I haven't forgotten either and

48

the law has a very long memory when it comes to child-molesters. How do you fancy going on the Sex Offenders' Register? I think we should meet.'

'I . . . I'm going to hang up.'

Sarah hardened her voice. 'You can if you want to, but that would be a very bad move.'

The next pause was even longer. 'What do you want?' he said at last. 'Money?'

'Not if you're a good boy.'

'Sex?' he said hopefully.

'In your dreams!' Sarah snapped. She looked down at the notes again. 'Tomorrow evening, take the Tolbooth road. About five miles out, there's a minor road on the right, posted "Craigmile Cottages". Half a mile in, there's a flat area of waste ground on the left. Be there at seven. Have you got that?'

'I've got it. But—'

'No buts. Be there or the next call you get will be from the police.' Sarah killed the mobile phone and handed it back to Alice. Her hand was shaking. She was not aggressive by nature and the sound of Gordon Watkins's voice had revived memories which she had hoped were dead.

Alice kept them at work the following morning until the cottage was once again in pristine condition, the laundry was up to date and the inside of the van was fit for a lady to travel in. Tod had suggested that any close study of the supermarket premises should be left until they had the plans in their hands. With time to kill, the four took a walk along the beach where, in a brisk wind but gentle sunshine and with only the oystercatchers for company, they searched the tide-line for driftwood, shells and dead starfish. Old, forgotten joys made a tentative return. It was an interlude of carefree pleasure and a return to an innocence close to that of childhood. Once, Alice, turning to the figure beside her, was momentarily surprised to find Tod there instead of her father.

They ate early. On their previous visit to the super-market, Alice had been tempted by a loss leader to buy a box of Spanish red wine. The girls each took pride in their culinary skills and Tod, in particular, was beginning to appreciate a regime which rose above their accustomed convenience foods and carry-outs. He became enamoured of the alliance of oatcakes and Cheddar cheese with the red wine and had to be persuaded away from the table when Alice decreed that the time for departure was approaching.

Despite the help of a brilliant moon, Alice, in the restored passenger seat, had some difficulty in finding the place where a now-forgotten boyfriend had brought her for a sustained but unsuccessful attempt on her virtue. However, it was barely seven when the van pulled up on the hard ground in the black shade of a stand of conifers and the area was deserted. Foxy killed the lights. They waited. Alice was beginning to feel a looseness in her mid-section and she decided that the life of a blackmailer might not after all be roses all the way.

In a few minutes, a mud-stained four-by-four pulled up close to the van but beyond the shadows and out in the broad moonlight. Its lights died. After an interval, a figure emerged from the driver's door and stood uncertainly. Alice nudged Tod. 'Go and make sure that he's alone,' she whispered.

Tod touched Foxy's shoulder. 'You come too, in case he isn't.'

'And make certain that he doesn't have a hidden tape recorder,' Sarah said.

The two men emerged from the van and into the moonlight. The effect on the dark figure was electric. It jumped, span back towards its car, decided that there was insufficient time for an escape by that means and turned again to run. Then, realizing that Tod was on one side of him and Foxy on the other, it produced a roundhouse swing which caught Tod on one ear. But Foxy got a grip from behind and Tod imprisoned the kicking legs. Tod patted him over and between them they lifted the figure into the back of the van. Tod followed it in but Foxy got into the driver's seat.

'He's alone,' Tod said, 'and if he has a recorder he's hidden it where the sun doesn't shine.'

Alice put on the interior light. By its feeble glow, they studied the young man. He was, as Sarah had said, thin. His rimless glasses were askew. He was breathing heavily and salivating with nerves. The girls had followed most of the action through the open door. 'What the hell got into you?' Sarah asked. 'You only came for a chat.'

Gordon Watkins took some seconds to calm himself and regain his voice. 'Thought I was going to be mugged, didn't I?' He straightened his glasses and resumed nursing his fist. 'I was expecting to meet a girl I used to know and two men come rushing at me. What was I supposed to think? I've hurt my hand.' Terror was turning to mild indignation.

'You haven't done my ear a lot of good,' Tod retorted. 'Glaikit headbanger!'

'You're not going to be mugged,' Sarah said. 'Not just yet, anyway. I don't know what will happen in prison. They go hard on sex offenders, I believe.'

Gordon's expression went from indignation back to fear. 'How much do you want?'

51

'More than you've got,' said Sarah. 'But we're not looking to you for money, not if you help us out in another way. We just want a little favour. Do it and we'll forget all about your naughty games.'

Gordon blinked. This was not what he had expected. 'Help you out how?' he said at last.

'Your firm built the Fineway supermarket,' Tod said. 'The original plans will still be around. We want copies of the plans of the office area. Large scale. One to fifty would do. Structural and electrical. And we'll want a blank works order.'

Gordon seemed to be reassured rather than shocked. 'The plans might be missed but I could photocopy bits.'

Alice took a decision. 'The area around the manager's office would do.'

'I could do that. I have a key to the firm's offices on me.'

'All right, then,' said Tod. 'Go and do it.'

'Hang on a moment and let me think. The cleaners will be all over the place and if I go in later and switch lights on somebody's bound to see and how could I explain that? No, I'll do it tomorrow.'

Sarah looked at him as sharply as she could in the fading light of the overhead bulb. 'You're not getting cold feet?' she asked sharply.

'Of course I've got cold feet. But I'll do it. Can't afford not to, can I? No, I'm just being careful.'

Alice could only approve of his caution. 'Meet us again tomorrow night, then,' she said. 'We'll wait for you in the supermarket car park. And, remember, if you ever say a word about this to anybody at all, you'll find yourself in court.'

'I'm not daft,' Watkins said. Now that he had been offered a way out, his confidence was returning by the minute. He shifted in his seat. Tod opened the back door of the van.

The overhead bulb dimmed for a moment.

'Bugger it!' Foxy said. 'We need one more bit of help before you're off the hook. Give us a jump-lead start.'

'You think he'll do it?' Foxy asked as he drove back into the town.

'Of course he'll bloody do it,' Tod said. 'It's not as if we'd even asked for something that cost him, not like cash or a share of his favourite bird. He just photocopies a few bits of plans and hands them over. I bet he makes damn sure his fingerprints aren't on them. He won't want them traceable back to him if we blow it.'

'We mustn't blow it. Don't even think that we might.' Alice, looking through the windscreen and alerted by a change of pace, noticed that they had left their previous route for a side street. 'Where are you going now?' she asked.

'I don't know.' Foxy turned his head to study a Transit van parked in a front garden. He declutched and revved the engine and the van's lights brightened but after a good look he drove on. 'I'll know it when I see it. I need a new battery.'

'You won't find any of the tyre, battery and exhaust places open at this time of night,' Sarah pointed out.

They rounded a corner dominated by a church and entered a street of mixed houses and shops. 'Chrissake, do you know what a new battery costs?' When he mentioned a price, Sarah was silenced.

'Can't you get a second-hander?' Alice asked.

''Course I could. Trouble with second-handers is you don't know the one you get isn't as bad as the old one, or worse. Couldn't be much worse,' he admitted, 'but a bit. I'm looking for another big enough vehicle, parked somewhere dark and quiet.'

'Well, you can drop us at some distant pub while you do the dirty deed,' said Alice. 'I'm not going to fall foul of the law for the sake of a battery.'

'That's OK. Tod can come with me. It'll be quicker with two.'

'I suppose,' Tod said. 'But what we should've done was for Sarah to take young Gordon into the bushes while you did a swap for the battery out of his Range Rover.'

'Definitely no way,' Sarah said. She sounded genuinely scandalized.

'Why not? You've been there before?'

'And I'm not going there again. Not with him. He gave me the shivers sometimes. He seems to have improved a bit, but not enough. I gave you what you needed to bring him to heel and that's my contribution. And don't dare to give me any of your but-you-saids.'

'Well, pardon me for breathing,' Tod said.

Foxy looped and turned around the back lanes and rear car parks until he had a mental picture of the most likely prospects. Alice and Sarah were dropped near a brightly lit café and warned to listen for the van's two-note horn. The café was a place of steam and plastic but at least it was warm and bright and the tea was good. They nursed a cup of tea and a sweet cake apiece. The passing time seemed more than would have been needed for a simple substitution of batteries.

'What do you reckon?' Alice asked. 'Are we building the nucleus of a competent gang? Or surrounding ourselves with incompetent idiots who'll drop us in the you-know-what?'

'The way I see it,' said Sarah, 'we've collected three blokes who're each bright enough in their own lines but have about as much common sense as a black pudding outside it. But that doesn't matter, because your modus operandi is to spell it all out, tell them what to do if this happens and that happens and don't forget to blow your nose—'

Alice was abashed. 'I'm not that bad, am I?'

'That's how you are, but I wouldn't call it bad. They trust you. And you've got to get even more so because, if anything went wrong that you hadn't thought of, they mightn't know what the hell to do. You know the old motto – "When in danger or in doubt, Wave your arms and rush about".'

Alice had never seen herself as the bossy type, but she had never before had a gang to boss. The thought kept her mind occupied while Sarah prattled on. The horn's double note never sounded, but at last Foxy appeared outside the window and beckoned.

'Oh, dear God!' Alice said softly as they got up. 'He can't start the van.'

'Or he's crashed it.'

'Or Tod's been arrested.'

As they exited, Foxy beckoned again, held a finger to his lips and set off for the street corner at a pace which had them struggling to keep up. The side street was narrow and dark and the van was parked without lights, tucked almost into a warehouse gateway. Foxy fairly leaped into the driver's seat. As soon as the rear doors were closed, the engine fired – much more willingly than before – and they were off. The headlamps seemed to blaze. Alice was immediately struck also by a change to Foxy's driving style. He was usually a slapdash driver, given to thrusting his way through traffic and leaving it for others to avoid a collision; but now he was moving briskly while staying strictly within the precepts of the

Highway Code. His route, also, did not seem to be the most direct but to cut through dark lanes and byways.

'You got a battery, then,' Sarah said. 'So what went wrong?'

'Nothing,' Foxy said. 'Well, not a lot. Only Tod bust his hand.'

'Don't think it's bust,' Tod's voice said out of the darkness. 'Just bruised. But I'm getting a cauliflower ear.'

They passed a street lamp and Alice saw that Tod's hand was tucked into the front of his denim jacket. 'How?' the girls said together.

'There was this camper-van parked behind a quiet pub,' said Foxy. 'Only one other vehicle in the car park and no more than just enough light to swap batteries. Seemed just the ticket. We went at it quietly, just in case there was somebody around to hear. What we didn't know was that some guy – the owner, maybe – was having it off with his bird inside. They must have been sleeping afterwards, because I got out their battery and put it into this van and I was just about to install my old battery in their van when they came to life. Either they heard me or he tried to switch on his lights and got nothing, because suddenly the door slammed open and he came leaping out. He was stark bollock naked. I don't know what happened after that because I jumped in here bloody quick.'

'Leaving me to fight the good fight,' Tod said grumpily. 'What happened was his bird jumped out after him and she was damn near as naked as he was.'

'Topless?' Alice asked in spite of herself.

'Other way. Bare-arsed. The bloke came running at me so I lamped him one and he sat down hard and I ran round the van and jumped in. As we took off, he got up and jumped into his driving seat, but without a battery connected he wasn't going anywhere fast. If he hadn't been in such a bloody hurry coming out he could have saved himself a doolander on the jaw, but I'd have had time to hook him up to my old battery and he might have been able to give us a chase.'

'What was that bang as I drove off?' Foxy asked.

'The bird threw something. A rock, I guess.'

'Whatever, it must have made a dent. So the van would be easier to describe to the cops. But I can bash it out all right. I'll call at a likely looking garage for masking tape and wet-or-dry paper and if it's dry enough and calm enough we'll do that spray job tomorrow. We'd better check that battery over to make sure that that other driver's number isn't marked on it.'

'They didn't get your registration number?' Alice asked.

'In that light and during all that schemozzle? Not a chance,' said Foxy.

Alice began to chuckle. 'We've just pulled off our first successful crime,' she said.

'Nah,' Foxy said into the windscreen. 'You using your mum's boss's credit card, that was our first crime. Yours, anyway.'

Alice stopped laughing

Chapter Five

The weather, for once, decided to he helpful. The new day came in calm, dry and warm – as good as you could hope for, so Foxy said, for satisfactory outdoor spraying. An hour was spent in knocking out and filling various major and minor dents in the bodywork and then the two men settled to cleaning and rubbing down the van's exterior. By the time their supply of aerosols was exhausted, several thin coats of black cellulose had been applied to the lower half of the van. In the afternoon Foxy, who had been caught up in enthusiasm for restoring his van's appearance, walked several miles each way to the nearest service station for an aerosol of red cellulose, leaving Tod to rub down and polish the new paintwork and to prepare the wheels. By dusk, the van, though still looking noticeably second-hand, was unrecognizable in two tones, white over black with red wheels, and Foxy was talking about a replacement engine and even seat-covers.

'It's rough,' Tod said, 'but at least it's different.'

The satisfaction of a job well done had given the men an appetite and they followed up their generous portions of chicken casserole with repeat helpings of fruit and ice cream. 'If you eat like this,' Sarah said severely, 'you'll soon be too fat to get into the van at all.'

'And we'll run out of money,' said Alice.

'The way you keep us at it, we'll never get fat,' Tod said. 'Anyway, we'll soon be rich.'

'Don't count your chickens,' Sarah advised him. 'Just eat them and be thankful.'

The supermarket was still open. Traffic was declining when they arrived as closing time approached, but the floodlights still fired a harsh glow over the building and car park. Tod dismounted and took an apparently casual stroll around the building.

As the last customers were being ushered out and the interior lights died, Gordon Watkins's four-by-four swept in and circled the car park doubtfully. Tod got out and raised a hand and the Range Rover parked beside them. Foxy wound down his window, but Watkins knocked on the rear door and climbed inside as soon as Tod opened it. He groped for a seat in the darkness. 'Here's what you asked for,' he said, holding out a large envelope until somebody took it.

Tod asked, 'Anybody out there?'

'Not within fifty yards.'

Tod put on the interior light, blinking in the unaccustomed brightness, and took a quick look at the contents of the envelope. 'Looks OK,' he said. 'All right. You're off the hook for the moment.'

Gordon Watkins was quivering with excitement so that his rimless glasses twinkled in the poor light. 'Listen,' he said. 'I know you've got a good caper going. Nothing else makes any sense. And I want a part of it. I need money as much as the next man, probably a damn sight more.'

'What do you need money for, all of a sudden?' Sarah asked. 'You used to be loaded.'

'I never said I was clever as well. I've been gambling and I've got debts. Now they're getting heavy about it and they mean business. They can get rough. I was becoming desperate. I was beginning to think about robbing a building society or something. Equal shares with you, that's what I want. One fifth. It's my turn to say, "Or else!"' His voice quavered but there was a new determination in it.

'Or else what?' Tod said contemptuously. He switched the overhead lamp off again. 'You're in no position to make threats.'

The younger man managed to find a laugh. It was meant to sound carefree but it was slightly hysterical. 'I am, you know. If I went to the police and said, "All right, so I was a bad boy about ten years ago but I can put you onto a gang that's planning to rob the supermarket," they wouldn't push the other thing.'

'Except that we'd abort whatever we're thinking of and you'd be left with your balls in a sling,' Foxy said over his shoulder.

'I could wait until you'd done the job and then point to you.'

'And you think we wouldn't drag you down with us?' said Sarah.

'Hold your fire,' Alice said. 'Stay cool, everybody. If what we want's in this envelope, Gordon's been useful. And he can be useful again.'

'That's true,' Tod said. 'I was wondering how to get past the watchman and borrow a Stihlsaw out of one of the sheds on the building site.'

'I could do that,' Gordon said. 'No problem at all.'

'Then I vote we let him join the club, for this one caper only.' There was a reluctant murmur of assent.

'Well, all right,' said Alice. 'But, Gordon, your next contribution is financial. We have to live and buy fuel for the next few days. Give me your wallet. You're being mugged, after all.'

'Think of it as a sprat to catch a mackerel,' Sarah said.

Alice held the wallet up to the back window and, in the light of a nearby lamp, relieved it of three new twenty-pound notes before returning it.

'It had better be a bloody good mackerel. That was my gambling stake,' Gordon grumbled.

'You're better without it – you'd only get deeper into hock. Come and join us tomorrow night after your work,' she said. 'We'll even feed you. By then we'll know if the job's on or not.'

'Hey!' Foxy said. 'You're not going to tell him how to get to you-know-where?'

'Why not?' Alice said. 'He's seen our faces, he knows Sarah and he's seen me before. We have to trust each other now.'

They waited nearby, bickering listlessly, to see at what time the car park lights were extinguished. As a result, they were very late in returning to the cottage and Tod resolutely put the photocopied drawings away. In the morning he studied them with care and then went for a walk along the beach, muttering to himself. He ate his lunch in thoughtful silence. Foxy shrugged and went back to titivating his van. The others gave the plans some consideration, each from their own viewpoint, but were content to leave the question of physical entry to Tod.

Gordon Watkins arrived in the early evening. He gave the interior of the cottage an uninterested glance and then looked round the four faces. 'Well?' he said. 'Is it on?'

'Slow down,' Tod said. 'It looks possible. But there are some rough edges to smooth out.'

Alice broke into a flurry of talk. 'Everybody sit,' she said. 'I didn't spend the last hour cooking to see it congeal. The supermarket will still be there. Foxy, pour wine.'

Foxy decanted Spanish red wine from a supermarket box into five glasses, three of them plastic and none matching, while Alice served soup. Pork chops were followed by sticky toffee pudding. Only when the meal was finished and the table had been cleared would Alice allow the conversation to turn to the subject at the forefront of everybody's mind.

Tod spread the photocopies over the table. 'I don't know what the idiots were thinking of,' he said. 'It isn't a safe at all. They built a strongroom with a door fit to go into a bank and they put it against an outside wall. When I saw the outlines of the columns as the wall dried out, I thought that the panels in between might be cavity brickwork, but they're not even that. According to this, they're just six inches of foam concrete, roughcast on the outside and plastered inside. They were built as drawn?' he asked Gordon.

'There was no change to the specification,' Gordon said. 'I checked the final measurement myself.'

'And you could borrow a Stihlsaw?'

'No problem. I could have a choice of three.'

'One will do. And there are no outside sensors. I could clear an opening through this in about ten minutes,' Tod said. 'But it wouldn't be quiet. Allow another ten for finding and moving what we want.'

'There's a factory backs onto the car park,' said Foxy.

'That's the printing works,' Sarah said.

'I saw a watchman doing the rounds. The cops would be all over us within that time.'

'Not necessarily,' Gordon said after a pause. 'Suppose somebody went to the watchman just before you started and showed him a works order from the supermarket to

McTaggart and Campbell, or from them to a foreman, instructing some cutting ready for a plumber to start work next day. Opening up to get at a leaking pipe, say.'

'You could do that,' Tod said.

Gordon shook his head emphatically and his voice climbed up the scale. 'I'm not going to show my face. An employee of the building firm producing a faked works order? They'd be onto me in a flash and I wouldn't have a leg to stand on. But I can give you a photocopy of a blank order form. You can fill it out for yourself. That way nothing can be traced back to me.'

'That seems reasonable. You'll have to do that bit,' Alice told Tod. 'You look more like a foreman or a supervisor than Foxy does. Borrow a suit from Gordon.' She paused and looked from on to the other. 'No, it would never fit. But clean working clothes and a hard hat should be convincing enough.'

'Even if that takes care of the watchman,' Alice said, 'there's almost bound to be somebody else sees or hears you at work and runs to the phone. The police are only a mile up the road. They'd be there well within twenty minutes. Unless . . .'

'Unless what?'

'Unless they had already had a dozen phone calls about crashes and break-ins and pub fights and hit-and-runs and things, so that what cars were available were all over the place and they didn't know what to believe first.' She paused for breath. 'We could do that with Gordon, from call boxes.'

'That's damn good,' Tod said. 'There are still one or two bits to iron out, but I think we're getting there.'

Alice had provided herself with a pencil and paper. 'Don't let me forget that this and the plans will have to be burned before we go ahead, but let's make a timetable and a shopping list. This is Thursday, right? Let's time it for this coming Sunday night. No point hanging around, waiting until we run out of money or some damn meter-reader turns up here. Tomorrow, we buy aerosols, ready to change the van's colour again. And some latex gloves. What else?'

'I heave the Stihlsaw and a couple of spare discs into the boot of my car,' said Gordon. 'There are men due to lay paving on one of our smaller sites and I can make damn sure that they'll have a use for it on Monday. I'll bring it out to you.'

Tod had been scowling at the drawings. 'Somebody,' he said, 'goes to see the boss-man in his office. I want to be told that the layout is just what it says here, especially the width of the strongroom and the position and angle of the sensors. I mustn't get it wrong. If a hot and spinning disc comes out in the office within the arc of the sensors, in about five seconds the alarms will be telling the cop-shop all about it. One of you girls can go and ask for a job.'

'Not me,' said Sarah. 'I worked there once before and he'd remember me.'

'You're sure you're not flattering yourself?' Alice suggested.

'Dead certain positive. He tried to grope me and I kneed him where it hurt.'

'If he's that way inclined, he probably gets kneed every day of the week.'

'Not as hard as I did it. Another thing,' Sarah said. 'The supervisor often interviews checkout and shelf-stacking applicants in her own cubbyhole. But you did most of a course at the Commercial College. If you asked to see the manager about a clerical job, he'd see you in his room.'

Alice cast up her eyes. 'I just knew that I'd end up as a human sacrifice. All right. Into the lion's den. But I don't want to be recognized again either. I live around here and I don't want to have to emigrate.'

'If we put you in a shorter skirt and pad out your bust, he won't notice anything else about you,' Sarah said. She made a two-handed gesture in the air. Gordon looked dazed. 'We can dress your hair differently and change its colour temporarily with one of those shampoos. Where's the nearest chemist?'

'Near the filling station I walked to yesterday,' said Foxy.

'You can get some more exercise, first thing tomorrow,' Sarah said. 'Alice, make a note. Then, if we change your makeup and you wear one of my tops, your own mother wouldn't recognize you.'

'She'd better not,' Alice said. Mentally she checked her story. There would be no sense in letting Tod and Foxy know her true status; they might decide that reversion to the kidnapping plot was the better option. While other heads were down, she gave Gordon a warning glance. 'Not that she'll get the chance – she does the shopping at Anderson's. All right, I suppose I have to pull my weight. Let's get on. I want to finish the timetable and start thinking about everything that could possibly catch us out. We've got to think ourselves into the minds of an investigating policeman.'

'It's going to be a long night,' said Tod.

'If we get it wrong,' Alice said, 'it'll be a damn sight longer . . .'

'In the clink,' Sarah finished for her. 'Let's just think about it for a minute before we decide to go ahead.'

They thought about it.

A scarlet-haired Alice emerged rather precipitately from the back door of the supermarket, her sudden jump

provoked by a hand up her short skirt and a finger danger-
ously close to her bottom. Clever application of makeup
by Sarah had given her the appearance of hollower cheeks
with higher cheekbones and larger eyes, and had added
prominence and a slightly pink tip to her nose. The short
skirt and the dimensions of her bust were now sufficient
to ensure that male eyes, at least, would not go straight
to her face. If her father saw and recognized her now, she
thought, he might be justified in thinking that she looked
like a tart.

She was still blinking in the glare of the setting sun
when she heard the panic bolt being angrily reset on the
door behind her. The van was waiting a few yards away
and there were no strangers nearby. She arrived with a
patter of furious footsteps, climbed into the back and
resumed her customary seat, which she had made more
comfortable with a cushion purloined from the cottage.

'Nasty, fat little pig,' she said, 'with hands everywhere.
Being robbed is the least of the things I wish on him.
Any supermarket that stoops to employ him deserves
to be raided, then knocked down and salt sown on the
foundations, or whatever it is that it says in the Bible.
Let's get on back so that I can wash this stuff out of my
hair and the memory of him off the rest of me.'

Sarah had taken over the front passenger's seat. 'Unclench
your fists and relax,' she said. 'I did warn you.'

'The half was not told unto me,' Alice retorted. Her
experiences had put her in a biblical mood. 'He's a
craphound and it's a wonder that he keeps any female
staff at all.'

'Hold it, Foxy!' Tod growled. 'Alice, tell me what you
saw now, quick, before your memory gets unsure.'

'All right.' Alice thought back. 'It all looked pretty
much like the drawings. A clerkess took me along a short

passage towards the back door, the one I came out of. I turned left into the manager's office and there was a short piece of passage with the strongroom door on my right. It was just over seven floor tiles long.'

'Hold it a minute.' Tod held up a floor plan to the fading light coming through the small rear window and read off a dimension. He produced a stump of pencil and jotted a sum on the margin. 'That's fine. A standard floor tile. It was the same size of tile right through?'

'It looked the same to me. There was no window, no natural light at all, just tubes. And the strongroom came out twelve and a bit tiles from the outside wall.'

'That checks. What about the alarm sensors?'

Alice tapped the plan. 'Just one, in this corner. If it's any help, Mr Farquhar was sitting with his back to the outside wall. Whenever I moved, the sensor clicked and showed a little red light, but when he leaned back it didn't.'

'Ah! So if I accidentally break through into his office, it shouldn't register. Great! I think that's about it. Home, Foxy.'

'Don't you want to know about the back door?' Alice asked.

'I don't think so,' Tod said. 'You came out through the back door, just as I asked, and I got a look. If I go by the plan, I won't be more than a few inches out.'

The van moved sedately out into the street.

'Did you get your CV back?' Sarah asked Alice.

'He kept it. He said he'd write to me. It doesn't matter about the CV, even if they connect the mythical Mary McLure with somebody casing the joint. It was all invented anyway, even the name and address, I ran it off without touching the paper and I handed it to him with my left hand which has clear nail varnish over the tips.'

Foxy made a left turn very carefully. The attention of the police would be even less desirable than usual. When the traffic had sorted itself out he spoke over his shoulder. 'He'll make the connection all right if his letter comes back to him marked "Address unknown" or something like.'

'It won't matter if he does,' said Alice. 'I almost bumped into a girl who had been my best friend at school. She looked right at me without the least sign of recognition. Even if I show up on a security camera, nobody would know me.'

'That's what you get for having a very ordinary sort of face,' said Foxy.

'Well, look who's talking,' said Sarah. 'You'd better go for cosmetic surgery before you make remarks like that. You know about people and glass houses?'

'Hey! Screw the bobbin!' Foxy exclaimed. 'Don't get your knickers in a twist. She's better looking than you are, anyway.'

Sarah emitted an unladylike snort. 'You'd better get your eyes seen to at the same time.'

Gordon Watkins arrived at the cottage direct from work. Alice had promised to feed him again if he brought wine, so he came with another box, of claret. His manner, now that he was dealing with practical rather than social acts, was more confident. Alice thought that he might still jump at shadows, but not so high.

'The Stihlsaw's in the boot of my car,' he said, 'with a couple of spare discs, just in case.'

'Fetch it out and let's have a look at it,' Tod said.

Gordon went back to his car and fetched the Stihlsaw – a two-stroke motor driving a rotary disc of diamond particles set in a compatible alloy. By the light spilling out of the door, Tod, with the ease of familiarity, checked that there was ample fuel in the small tank. He opened the valve on the filler-cap and pulled the starting cord. The little motor fired immediately. He stopped it after a few seconds. 'Seems OK.'

'Will that really cut through a concrete wall?' Sarah asked.

'It's only foam concrete blockwork. I could cut through it with a penknife, only it would take too long. Dead easy. Matter of fact,' Tod said, 'I can't think of many things this wouldn't cut through. Did you bring lamps?' He led the way back indoors.

'Two,' Gordon said. 'You'll need them if you're going to wait until the car park lights go off. And there's goggles and a clipboard with a photocopy of a blank works order. Do you need a hard hat?'

'Got one,' said Tod.

'A mobile phone?'

'I have one,' said Alice.

They settled around the table. 'I'll leave you my mobile number,' Gordon said. He looked around the other faces and drew courage from some mysterious source. 'I've been thinking. We can't be sure what time the car-park lights will go off or when you'll have finished speaking to the nightwatchman at the factory. I suggest that Tod has your mobile and Alice and Sarah come in my car. We'll wait somewhere at the far end of the town, in case they can pinpoint the payphones. When Tod's ready to start, he phones me and passes a code message and we start making calls to the police. We can report fights, fires, crashes, almost anything but we'll be vague enough about addresses to keep them searching around. When Tod's finished, he passes another code word and I bring Sarah and Alice back here.'

'That sounds all right,' Alice said. 'But you needn't come all the way out here in the small hours of the morning. We could meet the van on the outskirts of the town.'

'No, thank you very much,' said Gordon. 'I want the Stihlsaw back ready for Monday morning.'

'I bet you do,' Foxy said. 'But you could get it back at the same time. What you really want is to have the girls with you until we meet and divvy up.'

Gordon produced a twisted smile. 'Perish the thought,' he said. 'Like you said, we have to trust each other.'

Chapter Six

On the Sunday, the mist and drizzle made a return. They drove to the rendezvous with the tyres hissing over wet roads and the wipers beating out their hypnotic rhythm. 'All to the good,' Tod said. 'Less visibility, muffled sound and all the nosy parkers at home in front of the telly.'

'You're sure you don't want one of us to come as a lookout?' Sarah asked. Alice nudged her and gave her a headshake.

'We've been over and over it,' Tod said in a tone of great patience. He was riding in the front for once. 'Let's stick to what we agreed. A lookout can't do a damn bit of good and might only arouse suspicions. If the cops nose around, we produce the works order and try to bluff it out. But if you do your stuff they'll be too busy to bother us. They won't bother about a couple of workmen at the back of the supermarket while there's rape and rammies being reported from the other end of the town.' He tried to sound calm, but now that the time was rushing at them he felt a knot in his stomach.

'Well, all right,' Alice said. 'But no violence, mind.' Now that they were on the move and their plans were in train, her own nerves seemed to have evaporated.

'If one young bobby turns up on his own and gets officious,' said Foxy, 'there might be a little roughhouse.'

That seemed reasonable. 'Well, only a very little,' Alice said.

Gordon's Range Rover was waiting in the shadows under the trees fronting an ancient church. He came to the van's window. All five said, 'Good luck!' Alice and Sarah transferred to the four-by-four. The van pulled away.

'I'll let them get clear,' Gordon said. 'We've got more time than they have. No point being seen driving in convoy.' He waited for several minutes before driving off, with strict attention to the speed limit.

In nearly two days available for preparation, during which their plans had been refined and streamlined to what they believed to be near perfection, Gordon had scouted the ring road and picked on a small shopping complex as ideally suited to their purpose. There were several public telephones in working order and within easy reach and the shops were surrounded by a maze of small streets which had been named with the evident intention of confusing the stranger or even the unwary local. He backed the car into a short cul-de-sac serving two or three small service industries. He placed his mobile phone on the dash and they began the wait.

At first there was activity to watch. The pubs were closing and people were walking home or running for the last buses. There were cars and taxis. At last all was quiet, almost dead, except for the occasional pair of lovers, walking entwined, oblivious to the weather.

'They should have started work by now,' Sarah said. 'You're sure that thing's switched on?'

'Certain.' Nevertheless, Gordon picked up his phone and switched it off and on again. The light in the panel was reassuring. 'And it's fully charged. I need to pay a little call.' He got out of the car and vanished.

'Nerves getting to him,' Sarah said. 'He always did pee

a lot when he got nervous. If we have trouble, he may be the weak link.'

Alice had had the same thought but there was no point letting morale slip. 'He only has to make a few phone calls,' she said. 'Anyway, men need to go oftener than women. The plumbing's arranged differently.'

Gordon returned. 'They could have been held up by almost anything,' he said. 'The watchman may have been one of those chatty devils.'

'Or suspicious,' said Sarah.

'Probably Tod's dropped my phone and trodden on it,' said Alice. 'Or else he can't start that contraption.'

'Stihlsaw,' Gordon said peevishly. 'It'll start first pull, I guarantee it.'

'I expect Foxy's done something bloody stupid,' Sarah said. 'He's as thick as a tar-barrel. Or maybe the police have got there.'

'Why would that matter?' Alice asked. 'They haven't done anything yet, not to interest the police, or we'd have had the phone call. Don't struggle to invent disasters.'

They were silent again as time oozed sluggishly on its way and imagination conjured up calamities ranging from the unlikely to the downright impossible. When the phone played a little tune at last, each of them jumped. Gordon grabbed up the phone, fumbled for several agonizing seconds and then answered it. When he disconnected, they could hear the smile in his voice. '"I'll be home soon,"' he quoted. 'So the action's just about to start.'

They left the car and separated, each carrying a piece of notepaper. The phone box allocated to Alice was a quarter of a mile back along the dual carriageway. She walked along the grass verge, feeling the drizzle on her face and the damp seeping through her thin shoes. By the time she reached it, Gordon would already have reported being mugged outside a pub, promising to wait for the police 'on the corner', and have hung up without specifying the corner.

Alice snapped on a pair of latex gloves, dialled 999, asked for the police and reported sounds of violence coming from a specific number in Albany Crescent. There was an Albany Road, an Albany Street, an Albany Lane, an Albany Circle and an Albany Terrace but the street map had shown no Albany Crescent. There was a fault on the line, a dull buzzing and a muffled tone. The operator had to ask her to repeat the message. With a little luck, that might explain any confusion. She hung up and waited, giving time for Sarah and Gordon to pass another message each. A police car went by, blue lamps flashing.

While she waited, she looked around. On the other side of the dual carriageway, a man was sitting on a bench. He was in shadow although he was silhouetted against moonlight beyond. He seemed to be looking in her direction. Alice had reverted to her usual appearance and she felt exposed. But, she told herself quickly, he could hardly be investigating anything to do with her. She turned her back and phoned again, lowered her voice, gave a fictitious name and a real address and reported that several men were behaving suspiciously behind the bank. The line was still bad.

Many minutes later, she saw Gordon's Range Rover approaching. She made sure that she had the notes safely in her coat pocket, placed her last call and, assuming a voice breathless with panic, complained that a man had been following her. She broke off to scream, 'No, leave me alone,' then dropped the phone to dangle on its cord, hurried to the car and was spirited away. Another police car passed them in the opposite direction – which, Alice told herself, probably accounted for the sum total of the night-time strength of the local constabulary.

She looked back. The man was still sitting on the bench but vanishing with distance. Probably some drunk, she told herself, trying to sober up before going home. Nobody else would sit on a bench in such weather, at two in the morning.

They travelled in silence. They were nearing the turn-off before Sarah said, 'It's been more than twenty minutes. Surely they should have finished by now?'

Nobody answered. There was nothing to say. Each was imagining a different series of disasters. 'They've probably buggered off with the money and left us to whistle for it,' Gordon said suddenly.

'They wouldn't do that,' Alice said, but in her heart she suddenly felt a pang. Gordon had put his finger on her secret fear. There was a limit to how far trust could be made to stretch. Well, she knew the number of Foxy's van and she could always give it to the police, anonymously.

'They might,' Sarah said. 'After all, what do we know about them? I wouldn't trust either of them as far as I could spit.'

They arrived in front of the cottage. It looked naked and lonely in the car's lights without the van parked in front. Gordon looked at his watch. 'Either something's gone hellishly wrong or they've double-crossed us,' he said. 'Damn, damn, damn! Either way, I have to get a little sleep and get to my work in the morning, which isn't very far off now, and if the fuzz have gathered them up I'd rather not be here. Would either of you like to come with me? Or both? I could put you up.'

'You have a spare room, of course?' Alice suggested. 'Well, no.'

'You can go if you like, Sarah.'

'I'll wait with you,' Sarah said.

'I can trust you to see that I get my share?' Gordon asked anxiously.

'Eventually.'

'I suppose I'll have to trust you. If and when they do turn up,' Gordon said peevishly, 'give me a ring. I'll have to get the Stihlsaw back first thing. Or else report it stolen.'

'I'll phone you if I get my mobile back,' Alice said. 'If you don't hear from me, come here tonight.'

'All right.' They heard him draw in a deep breath. 'But you'd better be here. I can land you right in it, remember. And, as for me, I might be safer in the jug than waiting for my creditors to catch up with me.'

As soon as they were out of the car, Gordon backed, turned and drove off. They groped their way to the door and Alice worked the digital lock by touch alone. The familiar lights and warmth failed to cheer them. Alice, tidy as ever, hung up her coat before going to the kitchen cupboard and groping behind a small stack of tinned food. She produced a bottle of gin, still half full.

'Dad left this,' she said. 'I've been hiding it from the blokes but I think we owe ourselves a little something. There's no tonic. Will orange do?'

Slumped in two of the broken-down fireside chairs, they tried to unwind. 'I'm totally and utterly pooped,' Sarah said, 'but I don't think I have enough energy left to go to bed and there doesn't seem to be much point. We wouldn't sleep if we were expecting the cops to come knocking at the door at any moment.'

Alice yawned until her jaw cracked. 'I'm not expecting any such thing,' she said. 'Whether they've cheated us or been caught, they won't lead them here.'

'I wish I was as sure. I think Foxy would sell us out to get a better deal. If they've gone off with the dosh, what do we do? Turn up at home?'

It was a tricky question. Alice had been counting on an influx of cash. 'Let's treat that as a desperate last resort. At least we have a roof over our heads for a few months. Dad never comes out here until it's time to get the boat ready for launching, about March or April, and anyway he wouldn't be surprised to find us here. I don't suppose he'd mind particularly, provided we'd kept the place in good order and weren't sleeping with any blokes. We could get jobs of a sort.'

They finished their drinks. There seemed to be little else to do, so Alice poured two more.

'We'd need transport,' Sarah said.

'Between us, we could probably raise enough for a very cheap motor-scooter.'

They were beginning to accept that there would never be any money. They argued the pros and cons of a third drink apiece but Alice put the kettle on instead. It was approaching the boil when a murmur jerked them to their feet. It resolved itself into the familiar sound of the van's engine, but labouring slowly. They ran, stumbling with weariness, to the door.

The grey light of dawn was beginning to show. The van crawled closer and stopped. It looked low to the ground. Tod and Foxy emerged. 'Come inside before we freeze,' Alice said quickly.

Foxy locked the van carefully, a precaution which he had never previously taken. Under the lights, Alice saw that they both looked exhausted. 'Did you get the stuff?' she demanded.

'We think so,' Tod said.

'Think?' The kettle chose that moment to come to the

boil and begin its brain-numbing whistle. Sarah killed the noise quickly and filled the teapot. 'Surely you know,' Alice protested. 'And why didn't you give us the signal?'

Tod slumped into one of the fireside chairs. Alice managed to beat Foxy into the next most comfortable chair. Foxy leaned against the table.

'Long story,' Tod said. 'I'd kill for a cup of that tea. We were delayed. When I phoned, I got Gordon. So we met him at the big roundabout and gave him back the Stihlsaw. He's coming out this evening to see what we've got.'

Sarah started handing round mugs of strong tea. 'Well, what have we got?' she asked. 'Did you get through the wall? What was the delay? The watchman? Or did you get punctures? You seemed to be almost scraping the ground.'

'The watchman was no problem at all. The first delay was a camper-van in the car park. The same one that Foxy pinched the battery out of. The guy took his time. I suppose he was there for another bit of the same. When he'd finished and drove off, he took a damn good look at the van, so it was just as well we'd changed it or we might have had another rammy. Now we'd better change it again, because he'll go running to the police as soon as he hears about a break-in at the supermarket.

'As soon as he'd gone we got going. We cut through the wall, easy as butter, and came up against another wall – of boxes. The strongroom was just about full, stacked to the bloody ceiling, with locked metal boxes. Well, we'd no way of knowing which ones the money was in, if it was in any of them, and we didn't have time to force them all, so the only thing to do was to take the lot. And they were heavy, that's what took most of the time. And then the van was so loaded it was bumping along on the stops, so we couldn't go fast and we had to stick to the back streets and minor roads, because if the cops had seen us they'd have stopped us for being overloaded and then the fat would have been in the fire. That's what took the rest of the time.'

'And now my van's full of heavy metal boxes,' Foxy said, 'and we'll have to break into every damn one of them. But I'm not going to think about it until I've had a rest and got a breakfast inside me.'

'You still got that cordless drill in your box?' Tod asked. 'Better bring it in and put it on charge.'

'Can't,' Foxy said. 'It's under all those tin boxes.' He sounded pleased.

Each one of the four was eager to find out what they had managed to collect but, between exhaustion and letting down after the tension, they were almost asleep on their feet. Foxy was the first to stir. He got up and made for the kitchen corner.

The first scent of frying bacon was enough to rouse the others and set their mouths watering. Despite exhaustion and suspense, four hearty breakfasts were taken. After another interval of lassitude, Foxy hauled himself to his feet and made towards the door.

'Shouldn't you take a proper rest before handling sharp power tools?' Sarah asked.

Foxy shook his head and staggered slightly. 'Gone past my sleep,' he said thickly. 'Wouldn't be able to sleep any more, not knowing. Tod can sleep in if he wants.'

Tod yawned but struggled up. 'Want. But I couldn't either. I'm coming. Lasses can go back to bed.'

Sarah and Alice cleared the table and then ran out of energy. But bed seemed a long way away and the results of their efforts were about to be laid bare. They settled in the fireside chairs.

They expected to doze but sleep had fled. There must have been some moving of boxes within the van, because the cordless drill was brought in and put on charge. ('Not that it needs it,' Foxy said. 'It was fully charged when I put it away.') Then the metal boxes began to come into the cottage out of a steady rain. They were not absolutely consistent in size, shape or colour and had evidently been acquired from a number of sources, but they all seemed to have been intended as large cash boxes with individual locks. Each had a reference number stencilled on the side. ('You'd need that,' Sarah pointed out, 'to keep track of all the keys.')

'The weekend's takings,' Alice said drowsily, 'would have gone in last. You were emptying the strongroom from the back, so the cash would have gone last into the van again. So my guess is that it came out of the van first.'

'Could be,' Foxy agreed.

A discarded shower curtain was spread on the floor to catch any metal fragments. Then, while Tod continued to carry in box after box, Foxy fitted a bit to the drill and began drilling into the lock of the first box to have come in. The noise of the drill was mildly soporific. After a minute he said 'There!' and lifted the lid. The girls sat up.

'Credit-card slips,' Foxy said disgustedly.

'If I hunted through them,' Alice murmured, 'would I be able to find the slip from all that stuff I bought on . . . that credit card and tear it up?' She just stopped herself from mentioning her father.

'Wouldn't matter,' Sarah said drowsily. 'First, we've got them here anyway. Second, the transaction went to the credit-card company electronically.'

Alice lost interest again.

Tod seemed to be making heavy weather of carrying in the boxes but the others were more interested in Foxy and his drill. Foxy put the box aside and picked another at random from the small stack which was beginning to grow beside the door. Two minutes later he said, 'Bingo! Money!'

Sarah sat up. 'Much?'

'Coins, in rolls. You ladies can add them up.'

Wearily, Alice and Sarah moved to the table. Counting coins was at least a step in the right direction.

Foxy opened the next box. 'Neat packets of something,' he said, 'but it doesn't look like used banknotes. We'll put it aside.'

Next came more coins, which were again transferred to the table. It was followed by another box of the precise, rectangular packets. The sixth box at last produced a supply of grubby, crumpled, beautiful Scottish banknotes. They cried 'Yes!' in unison and shared the traditional high handclap.

The eighth and eleventh boxes repeated the bonanza. From there on, it was the paper bricks all the way. The notes produced a disappointing total. 'Eleven thousand, two hundred and something,' Sarah said disgustingly. 'Just over two grand apiece. Hardly life-changing, is it? Don't people use cash any more?'

'It'd keep us going while we pay back the Assistance people and find new work,' Tod pointed out.

'Somebody must have done a run to the night safe,' Sarah said. 'And sometimes people ask for cashback. What's in the packets? If it's drugs, we could still be in the money.'

Tod, his portering finished, had lowered himself carefully into one of the easy chairs. 'If it's drugs, I'm dumping it on the doorstep of the cop-shop. We don't want anything to do with it. Anyway, they're the wrong sort of shape. Let's take a look.' The opened boxes had encroached within his reach. He reached out for one of the mystery packets and slit the brown wrapper with a pocket knife. 'Bloody hell!' he said sincerely.

'What is it?'

'Does anybody know what a hundred-euro note looks like? If these are what I think they are, we've got a whole lot. Brand-new hundred-euro notes, about a ton of them.'

Chapter Seven

There was silence for a full ten seconds and then Tod said a very rude word under his breath.

'These are legal tender in Europe,' Foxy said. 'There must be millions. We could do what we said at first, go live in Spain.'

'Bugger Spain. We could go to Tahiti. Or the moon. What's the rate of exchange?' Tod asked. 'Around one and a half to the pound, give or take, isn't it?'

Alice was assailed by a feeling of panic, of events running away. 'Hold on,' she said. 'Stop and think for a minute. What the hell would about a ton of brand-new euros be doing in a supermarket strongroom?'

'Money-laundering, you think?' Sarah asked.

'Don't be daft. I'll bet you what you like that it's fake. Counterfeit. Slush. Call it what you like, you'll end up in the pokey if you try spending it. I bet you it's been prepared and it's waiting for the euro to become legal tender in Britain. Then they'd just dump them into general circulation before people became so familiar with the look and feel of the real thing that fakes would be spotted quickly.'

There was a gloomy silence.

'On the other hand,' Alice said at last, 'this must have a high value to whoever printed it. I suppose they'd push it out through their agents at – what? – about a third or a half of the face value, so they'd be expecting a very large profit at the end of the day. On yet another hand, it would be disaster for them if we took it to the police.'

Sample packets from different boxes were opened. Only the denominations varied.

'This is going to need some thinking about,' Alice said. 'Let's sleep on it. But first we'd better get it all out of sight before some meter-reader or council-tax valuer comes along.'

'We could move this stuff out into the boat,' Tod said. 'Who'd look there?'

Foxy yawned and stirred. 'I'm not saying you're wrong,' he said, 'but something else comes first. That punter in the supermarket car park took a damn good look at my van as he drove off. Not to look at the number plate, but wondering if it wasn't the van that got away with his battery. As soon as the news gets around that the supermarket was broken into, he'll be shouting to the cops about a black-and-white van with red wheels. We daren't go anywhere in it until I've changed the colours again. And I'll have to do it before word gets to the cops and they spread the word to all cars.'

'You won't be able to spray outdoors in this weather,' Tod said.

'No. But the job has to be done quick. I reckon I'll go back to the old barn where we went first. Come with me, Tod. I need somebody to help with masking and rubbing down or it'll take twice as long.'

Tod put his hands to the arms of the chair and then collapsed with a groan. 'Give me a break,' he said. 'You've gone soft, driving cranes and diggers. I had to handle the Stihlsaw, shift the concrete and then do nearly all the carrying of those damn boxes; and with one hand not much use I was doing all the carrying lopsided. I've done my back a whole lot of no good. I'm whacked.'

'Whacked or not, it's got to be done.'

'Not by me.'

'I'll come with you, Foxy,' Sarah said. 'I'm too keyed up to sleep.'

Foxy gave her a look, judging her capability, and then nodded. 'You're on,' he said.

The two left, yawning but still managing to bicker over Foxy's choice of colours.

Moving listlessly, Alice made sure that all the boxes were closed and then, with some difficulty, rebuilt them into a stack which could be covered by an old counterpane that she remembered once featuring on her parents' bed. There was still a little left in the gin bottle, so she mixed herself one last drink.

Tod was trying to relax in the chair but it was obvious that he was in some discomfort. 'Can you manage?' Alice asked him.

Tod moved his arms and winced. 'You'd think I'd know better by now. Pain's just nature's way of saying don't do that again, but when you've got to do it again, you do it and pay the price. It's arthritis. I knew I was going to have to accept a loss of money and get a desk job soon anyway, or one as a supervisor, maybe a site agent or a clerk of works. Working outside in all weathers gets you in the end.'

'Would you be better off taking the bed? I'll make do with the chair.'

He smiled wryly. 'You're a good kid. Yes, I think I would. They never make chairs high enough for a man to rest his head and neck.'

Alice was beginning to feel a motherly protectiveness

towards him. He was almost attractive when he was allowing his dependence to show. 'I'm quite good at massage. Have a hot shower and then I'll rub your back for you. Shall I help you up?'

'I can manage, I think.' He made several efforts before struggling to his feet.

Alice went into the bedroom. When they had gone out on the robbery, she had worn a good dress in case she had to bluff it out with the police. She had no wish to get her dress marked with talcum powder so, while Tod showered, she changed into one of the bathrobes.

Tod came through with a towel around his waist and subsided face-down with a groan on the bed. The bed was low and Alice found the position awkward. Rather than stoop and risk her own back, she knelt straddling Tod's lower back, sprinkled her own talcum over his shoulders and began work.

He was well muscled from his work. She sought out the small knots of fibrositis and worked on the long muscles, stretching and soothing them into relaxation. He jumped when she ran her fingers down his spine, checking that the vertebrae were in alignment. She dismounted and switched off the bedroom light. In the horizontal light coming through the bedroom door, the processes of his spine threw distinct shadows and she could see a break in the regularity. She applied pressure with her thumb. Tod yelped and jerked but she was rewarded by a tiny movement. The shadows were straight.

'Is that better?'

'I think so.'

A little later, she thought that he was asleep. The bathrobe had fallen open. With Tod lying face-down, she thought that it would hardly matter, but when she glanced to one side she saw that he was watching her in the dressing-table mirror. When he met her eye, he turned his head the other way in a gesture of modesty which she thought was characteristic. With two men and two girls living at close quarters, occasional revelations of lingerie or rosy flesh had been inevitable but, while Foxy had shown no objection to such fortuitous glimpses, Tod had modestly averted his eyes.

'That smells nice,' he said. 'It smells like you. You always smell nice. Ladylike.'

'Thank you, kind sir,' she said lightly. 'Now, is that really better?'

He moved tentatively. 'A whole lot better. You're a living doll.' She began to dismount again. He caught her hand and pulled her down gently beside him, turning to face her. 'You're not just gorgeous, you're kind and clever too.' He took her face in his hands and kissed her. He was stubbly but clean and he smelled fresh. 'How about it?' She became aware of a remarkable change in his mid-section, peeping through the towel. It spoke a message to some inner ear.

Alice might never previously have wholly surrendered to any of the various youths who had pursued her, but she was not totally inexperienced. Straddling Tod and working on his bare back, she had been aware of responses in herself which she knew to be the onset of desire. The unaccustomed drink combined with the exaltation from a crime successfully pursued had induced a heady sense of elation. She would have to part with her hymen some day, and that sacrifice might be a suitable climax to a remarkable period. After all the effort, the planning and the triumph, she thought, to go quietly to sleep would be like finishing an opera with a fart. Some grander chord was called for.

'All right,' she said. 'Three things. Be slow. Be gentle. And be careful.'

'Gentle, I can manage,' Tod said. 'Slow is all I could manage. Careful . . . if you bring Foxy's haversack to me, I can manage careful too.'

Her actual defloration, when it occurred, was less painful than she had been led to expect. It may be that all her attitudes were in a state of flux, or that she was so caught up in the emotion of the moment that she was barely aware of any discomfort. Moreover, her more adventurous friends had warned her that she need not expect to experience the fullest joy of sex on the first occasion. Sex, they had said with barely concealed complacency, was an acquired taste, but Alice, to her own amazement, responded intensely to every nuance of male musculature, contact and odour and soon found herself soaring effortlessly onto a cloud of intense physical pleasure where she lingered for what seemed to be a glorious eternity. Later, on the brink of sleep, while ecstasy subsided into mere pleasure, she decided that Tod must be a superlative lover or else she was gifted with an above-average libido. She rather thought that she might have responded to him with tigerish enthusiasm rather than the proper maidenly submission, but she was too contented to care about the niceties of sexual convention.

Daylight was fading again when Alice was awoken by the unfamiliar awareness of a warm body leaning against her, but there was no sign that the van was back. She felt relaxed but not sleepy although she could easily have slid back into sleep. But she rose quickly, showered and dressed. Sarah would be the last person to disapprove of the morning's events and Alice was quite unconcerned about Foxy's opinion, yet a beautiful experience would be sullied if the others even smirked at the knowledge of it. She woke Tod. He admitted that his back was very much improved but he still groaned as he dressed himself.

Alice tidied the bedroom hastily and then began preparations for a meal. Tod, who usually considered such chores to be woman's work, joined her at the sink and began peeling vegetables. The stack of boxes under the old counterpane seemed to take up half the room.

It seemed to Alice that she was spending her days waiting for a van which arrived late if at all. 'Those two are taking a hell of a time,' she said. 'Do you suppose the police have nabbed them?'

Tod paused, carrot in hand. 'Shouldn't think so. Another respray won't be a ten-minute job, even for a quick blow-over. They may even have had to go for more aerosols and then had to dry the van again. They've still got the lamps from last night. They'll turn up.'

'I suppose that's true. We'd better prepare something we can cook quickly when they show up,' Alice said. 'I don't want to make something that will spoil. There's a big pack of scampi in the freezer compartment. That with chips?'

'Sounds good to me.'

They finished their preparations and sat down with a glass of wine apiece. Tod fiddled with the transistor radio beside him and found some gentle music. He said, 'About what happened . . .'

'No need to say anything.'

'All right, I won't, then. Except that you were great. It was the best thing that ever happened to me. There. I've finished.'

Alice studied him for a moment. Another fallacy propounded by her peers had been that she would find herself imprinted with her lover. But, looking at him, she saw an adequate-looking, good-natured partner in crime with whom she had had a satisfactory sexual initiation. She was aware of a mild friendship; but if they had anything else, any deeper emotion, in common, she was unable to detect it. If Tod were to combust spontaneously before her eyes she would feel regret, but her heart would remain unbroken.

'Me too,' she said kindly. 'But it won't happen again.'

'I expected that,' he said.

They sipped their wine in companionable silence. 'Somebody will have spent the day in a tizzy,' Tod said.

Alice snapped awake. She had forgotten that, out there in the world, the repercussions of their act would be echoing between the supermarket, the police and the media. 'Mr Farquhar,' she said.

'Not just him. A supermarket manager couldn't get the paper, make the plates and print all those euros, all on his own. There's a lot of people behind him.'

'There's a paper-works down by the river,' Alice said, 'and a big printing firm just behind the supermarket. I suppose a few trusted employees working overnight could do the whole thing but there'd have to be somebody conducting the orchestra. A mastermind—'

She was interrupted by the sound of a vehicle and lights playing across the front of the cottage. She jumped to her feet and went to the nearest window. 'Here they are at last.'

'You're sure it's not the fuzz?' Tod sounded on edge.

'Not unless they've taken to using vans with squeaky springs.'

Sarah came in. She was alone. 'The job's done for the moment,' she said. 'Two tones of blue with silver wheels. It looks terrific if you don't get too close. At the moment, it's muddy with traffic grime and you couldn't tell that it hadn't come straight off the production line.

But that bloody Foxy wants everything done his way. He wants it all rubbed down and covered again. He's hell to work with.'

'Tell me something else that's new. What have you done with him?' Tod asked.

'I haven't done anything with him,' Sarah said indignantly, 'and I don't intend to. He was tired and annoying the hell out of me but I've gone past my sleep and I'm feeling quite fresh for the moment, so I drove back. And now he's sound asleep in the passenger seat and I was damned if I was going to carry him in, even if I could.'

'Let him sleep for a few minutes more,' Alice said. When she got up, Sarah took her chair and put her head back.

Alice put the pans on to heat. 'Where did you buy the aerosols?' she asked.

Sarah answered without opening her eyes. 'We went to four different places. Somebody might have remembered selling a whole lot. And we parked out of sight and took it in turns to buy them. I don't think we'll be remembered.'

'That's good,' Alice said. She wetted a cloth at the sink and went out into a steady drizzle. Foxy was slumped against the van's door and nearly fell on top of her when she opened it, but she pushed him upright and mopped his face with the cold cloth. He mumbled something unintelligible but opened his eyes and grunted.

'Come along,' Alice said kindly. 'You're home and there'll be a meal in a minute.'

She left him and re-entered the cottage. Her pans were heating nicely, the chip pan beginning to smoke. She began cooking the meal. Sarah seemed to be asleep. Foxy stumbled in and, seeing both the comfortable chairs occupied, lowered himself into one of the kitchen chairs, put his head down on the table and seemed about to doze off again. Alice laid the table around him.

Another set of lights swept across the windows. Alice looked out. The contours of the Range Rover were familiar. 'It's Gordon Watkins,' she said. 'Come for his pound of something.' She heard faint sounds as the others relaxed into somnolence again.

Gordon came in quickly, almost walking into the stack of boxes. He had come straight from a day's work after a night of inadequate sleep and Alice thought that if he got any thinner he might disappear altogether. 'Is that the same van outside?' he asked.

'It is,' Alice assured him. 'Sarah and Foxy spent all day spraying it.'

'I'd never have recognized it. So. How much did we collect?'

'One moment. Hush!' The music had finished on the radio and the news was on. Alice turned up the volume, above the fragrant sizzling in the pans. The break-in at the supermarket was reported, and the theft of 'a five-figure sum'. Mention was made of a two-tone van, white over black. The report stated that 'According to a police source, the gang was obviously well organized and professional.'

Alice and Tod exchanged a wink and a nod.

'But which five-figure sum?' Gordon asked plaintively. 'Ten thousand? Ninety-nine thousand? And what's in the boxes?'

'Nearer the first than the second,' Alice told him. 'There are some coins we haven't counted yet. In English notes, and a few Scottish, eleven thousand, two hundred and twenty-eight.'

'That's about what I expected,' Gordon said. 'Surely that didn't fill so many boxes? So what else did we get away with? A year's supply of Mars Bars? The manager's dirty laundry?'

Alice took pity on him. 'And,' she said, 'there's a few million quid, face value, in brand-new euro notes which we assume have got to be counterfeit. Now, there's still some wine in that box. Share it around the glasses.'

'Stone the flaming crows,' Gordon said. He picked up the wine-box. 'What are we going to do with the euros?'

'Discuss,' Alice said. 'Probably we should sleep on it and not do anything hasty. We're all too pooped out to think straight. Pour the wine.'

The transfer of the food to plates seemed to remind the company that they had eaten only irregularly in the previous night and day. Even Foxy roused himself enough to sit up and tuck in. They ate with small, pleasurable noises. There had been no time to cook a sweet and the weather was too cold for fruit alone, but Alice had thawed a frozen sweet from the supermarket and this, heated, with condensed milk for cream, followed the scampi.

The food seemed to give Alice a fresh buzz of energy. Thinking ahead had become a habit. She said, 'We'll have a shareout next. But tell me this. There may be some more to be squeezed out of the euros, but there may be danger. I mean, let's face it, we're rank amateurs compared to whoever organized the counterfeiting. Babes in the Wood. We only had to distract the police and hack our way through a wall; theirs was a much more sophisticated operation. It's only coming home to me now that, by a mixture of forward planning and good luck, we've pulled off out own coup and, if we stay careful, look like staying in the clear. But nobody managed to organize the paper, the engraving, the printing and storage of all those euros without having an organization with experience. There could be big men and hard boys. We'll have to walk very carefully. So tell me. Who wants to take their two grand plus and tiptoe quietly away?'

There was silence.

'Cupidity triumphs again,' Alice said. 'I assume that we're staying on here for the moment? Or does anyone want to move to a hotel or a bed-and-breakfast?'

Silence again.

'I'll take that as a yes followed by a no. Then I suggest that we each take two thousand, two hundred, and a share of the coins. The other two hundred and twenty-eight and some coins remain in the kitty. The cupboard is almost bare again and we'll soon have to do some serious shopping.' Alice got up and put the kettle on. 'Clear the table,' she said, glancing at a pencilled note, 'and then we want boxes eighteen, twenty-four, thirty-one, fifty and sixty-eight.'

'Just see me two hundred and keep my two grand safe for me,' Tod said.

'Oh no,' Alice said. 'No, thank you very much. I'm not taking responsibility for anyone else's share. I don't have any better hiding place than the rest of you. If you can't think of anything safer, go to a post office, buy a Jiffy bag and post the notes to yourself at some other post office marked "Poste Restante" or "Collect" or whatever one does. But, let me remind you, no chucking it around in clubs and pubs – that would be the one sure way to draw attention. If you must paint a town red, choose a town a long, long way from here.'

'Aye aye, skipper,' Sarah said.

Amid much yawning and bleary-eyed squinting, the notes and then the coins were sorted into denominations and then divided into five neat stacks. The five looked at each other, uncertain what to do or say. To break the silence, Gordon said, 'I'm for off. I'll be in touch. Keep your phone charged and switched on, Alice, so that I can reach you.'

'Don't bother to try it for about the next ten hours,' Alice said.

Chapter Eight

On wakening, Alice was surprised to find that, despite her afternoon nap, she had slept for another nine hours. The others awoke yawning but she felt ready to challenge the world.

Some disjointed discussion over breakfast failed to produce any more resolution than that the unpleasant Mr Farquhar at the supermarket was their only point of contact and that it would therefore be necessary to approach him on the subject of buying back the euros. Just who would make the approach, and how, remained undecided. Negotiations by telephone seemed to be the sensible option but face-to-face meetings would at some point become inevitable and at that stage there would be ample scope for getting it wrong. It was generally agreed that precipitate action might do more harm than good and that it might be better to leave things to simmer on the back burner.

Sarah volunteered to go shopping in some supermarket a long way away and, armed with a long list and a substantial sum from the kitty, she and Foxy drove off. 'Does that mean that they're getting along better?' Alice asked.

Tod considered. 'Likely not,' he said. 'It's Foxy's van, so he had to go. Sarah's got some money now and she's a woman, so I guess she wanted to get near the shops.'

Alice had nearly added herself to the shopping party.

She ignored Tod's last remark. 'A pity. We could do without the backbiting.'

'They don't really mind each other,' Tod said. 'It's just play-fighting, like puppies. I'll take a walk.'

Alice tidied the cottage, even to shaking out the bedspread which covered the stack of boxes holding the euros. Tod, who had never had much to do with the seaside before, had taken to walking along the beach, watching the seabirds, hunting for flotsam and bringing back souvenirs, some of which had to be banished to the outdoors before they stank the place out.

As soon as he was out of sight she extracted her fat wad of notes from under the pillow where it had disturbed her comfort for some of the night and looked for a more secure hiding place. She trusted her companions absolutely, she told herself, but there was no harm in being doubly sure. The others, it seemed, had thought along the same lines because her first choice of hiding place, behind the sink, was already occupied by a brown-paper parcel. Her second choice, a disused ceramic jar emblazoned COCOA, which she remembered her mother evicting from the house some years earlier, had also been called into use. A toilet cistern, so popular in fiction as a repository, was out of the question because the only toilet was of the chemical variety.

That thought, however, brought another in its wake. A spade leaned against the wall of the cottage, ready for the digging of holes for waste disposal. Foxy had already used it twice for that purpose although, at Alice's direction, at considerable distance from the cottage and its well. Alice looked outside. She could see Tod's figure, far away along the sand. There was the boat, but she could see no sign of the ladder and where the boat and trailer stood was an area of damp sand which would retain clear footprints. She washed out an empty tin and packed her money into it, reserving only a modest sum for immediate use. In front of the cottage, rank grass spread from the trees to the beach and anything buried there could be lost for ever, but there was one small patch of dry, sandy ground in which it would be easy to dig and to find again but which could be brushed over to show no trace of disturbance.

Again she had been anticipated. The second turn of the spade revealed a glass jar through which could be seen Bank of England notes. She refilled the hole with unnecessary violence and was rewarded by the sound of a satisfactory crunch. She found a bare patch behind a corner of the cottage and there her tin was laid to rest.

As she re-entered, her mobile phone, which she had left on the kitchen worktop, began to play its electronic tune. Gordon, of course. She lifted it.

But it was certainly not Gordon's voice which said, 'Alice, is that you?'

She said, 'Who's calling?'

'For Heaven's sake, darling, don't you recognize your own mother's voice?'

All that Alice could think of to say was, 'Mother, what are you doing at home on a Tuesday morning?'

'I came back to fetch some papers and the house phone was ringing. It was a friend of yours and when I told him that you were away from home and that I didn't have a new address yet he asked for your mobile number, so I gave it to him. I hope that was all right?'

'I expect so,' Alice said weakly. 'But please don't give it to anybody else without asking me first. Who was it?'

'I've no idea. You can't expect me to recognize all your friends' voices.' Her mother's voice took on a querulous note. 'Darling, I don't really blame you for running off like that, because by his own account your father was rather heavy-handed and he was sorry afterwards. But you could at least have contacted us again to let us know that you were all right.'

'I left you a note to say that I was all right.'

'And a very nice little note too, but it didn't tell us anything about where you were, who you were with and what you were doing.'

'That was because I wanted to be my own, grown-up person and not be treated as a child any longer.'

'I'm sure we'd be happy to know that you'd grown up a bit but we would like to know where you are. It was only when your friend phoned that I realized that I still had the number of your cellphone. Where are you? And is Sarah McLeod with you? She seems to have vanished at about the same time, leaving a note that was almost the clone of yours, and her parents are going scatty.'

'We're together,' Alice said. 'We're staying with friends.' Well, it was sort of true. 'We were both fed up about being badgered to make something of ourselves, so we're going to stay away until we've done it.'

'And you're not going to tell us where you are?'

'Not just yet.'

'There are some letters for you.'

'Leave them on the hall table.'

'But when will you be coming home?'

In one sense Alice had never quite left home, but she was not going to say so. 'Probably never.' (Mrs Dunwoodie made a sound of distress.) 'We want to get jobs or start our own little business. Then we'll get a flat together and you can come and visit us.'

'Oh.' Mrs Dunwoodie paused while she thought it over. 'And you're not short of money?'

It took an effort for Alice to keep the amusement out of her voice. 'We've agreed that we're not going to tap our parents for cash. That would be going back to Square One. I can assure you that we haven't gone on the streets. And we're not being kept by men.' What were her mother's other terrors? 'And I'm not smoking pot or drinking gin.'

'Oh, well, that's something, I suppose. I'll have to run, dear. I'm sorry if you feel that we were smothering you. Do please believe that we only wanted the best for you. You'll keep in touch?'

Alice crossed her fingers. It might not be possible. 'Yes, of course,' she said.

Her phone began to tinkle again just as Tod arrived back at the door. Alice answered it impatiently. It was her mother's frequent habit to reopen a phone call in order to deal with some trifle which she had forgotten during the original conversation.

'Alice, is that you?' The words were the same but it was not her mother's voice. It could be Gordon this time, but she had been caught out once and she had more sense than to offer names to unidentified callers.

'Who's calling?'

'That was a nice little stunt you pulled at the supermarket. Congratulations.'

It was definitely not Gordon. Alice flopped into the nearest chair. Her skin tingled. She could feel blood rushing from her face and her ears were singing. She could think of nothing to say. Thanks seemed inappropriate. 'I don't know what you're talking about,' she said at last. Gordon Watkins had said much the same thing. She knew now how he had felt.

'Yes, you do. Yours was one of the voices on the phone, diverting the police while your pals cut into the back of the strongroom.' It was a man's voice with

100

no discernible accent, sounding mildly amused. It was a pleasant voice, she decided, and remotely familiar although she could not place it, but its message was far from welcome. She lowered her head in case she should faint.

'Who are you?'

'I'm an old friend. I think we'd better meet and talk.' The voice could have belonged to any of a dozen acquaintances but she could not fit it to any one of them. 'Come to the lounge bar of the Cameron Arms at one o'clock. You know where it is?'

'I know it,' Alice said, 'but I can't make it by one. It's just not possible.'

'You'd better make it possible. I only have to mention your name and where you are to the police . . .'

Alice thought furiously and decided on a half-truth. 'Even to meet an old friend, that may be impossible because my car probably won't be back by then.'

'You only have to hop on the bus or take a taxi.'

So he had no idea where she was. Alice felt a little better. 'I can't make it by one o'clock,' she said firmly.

'How about later? Sixish?'

'I prefer a crowd. Make it seven. And if you're just buying time to set up something tricky, you'll be a sorry girl, believe me.' The tone was still friendly but there was steel in it.

Alice could, after all, have got to the Cameron Arms by one if she had skipped lunch, because the van was back by twelve. Sarah walked in with a box of groceries under one arm and brandishing a bottle of bargain-basement champagne in the other hand. 'That mad bugger Foxy wanted to buy a crate of this stuff for a real celebration, but his flatulence would have curled the furniture. I thought we could endure the after-effects of a quarter-bottle each, but I put the rest of it back.'

Foxy brought in a much larger carton. 'One bottle won't go far between the five of us, so let's open it now before Gordon turns up,' he said.

'Put it away in the fridge,' Alice said. 'I've something tell you.'

She told, for the second time, the brief story of the phone call. There was general consternation. The few available facts were rehashed, picked apart, analysed and mulled over during lunch and through the afternoon, but without any useful conclusions being drawn. At one point, Foxy suggested that they should take their winnings, abandon the euros and scatter, but Sarah rounded furiously on him, pointing that that would leave Alice facing disaster alone.

'Of course,' Tod said, 'whoever it is wants to meet you somewhere crowded in case you bring your gang with you – that's you and me, Foxy – and beat him up, for all the good that would do.'

'I doubt if it will come to that,' Alice said. 'I'll have to meet him and find out how much he knows and what he wants. I'll have to make it up as I go along but, as far as he's concerned, I was paid a flat fee for the telephoning and the euros are long gone, I know not where. There's no point showing him anyone else's face.'

'He may have seen us already,' Tod said.

'And he may not. He didn't know where we were or he couldn't have thought that I could just hop on a bus. It might be interesting to see whether he reacts to seeing you at long range and out of context. I suggest that you follow me in and watch from a distance. We'd better have some signals agreed. If he's careful, he may insist that I stay while he leaves. If you see me blow my nose, you'll

know that I know who he is and you can stay put. If
I – what? – if I get up, stretch and sit down again, I
want you to try to grab him outside – discreetly, mind,
we don't want anyone screaming to the cops. No signal
from me and you try to follow him without being spotted.
Got it?'

'Got it,' Sarah said. 'Blow your snout, we do nowt.
Big stretch, grab the wretch. You sit still, we're on his
heels. It doesn't quite rhyme,' she added apologetically,
'but it's near enough for a mnemonic.'

The Cameron Arms is a large and not unattractive hotel,
built of stone and roughcast and with a slated roof, on
one of the main arteries out of the town. It has a dozen
bedrooms, mostly given over to commercial travellers,
but it depends for its living on several large bars steadily
patronized by the many citizens who live within walking
distance, an adequate cuisine for business lunches and
dinners and a large room which can be used for a variety
of functions all aimed at encouraging the consumption of
alcohol.

At ten to seven that evening, after a cautious reconnais-
sance, Alice walked into the lounge bar. This was already
busy, but the customers were either couples enjoying an
evening out or groups of ladies returning from shopping
expeditions. In such company, she decided, she would
feel safe and no doubt the same thought had motivated
her 'old friend' in deciding the time and place. She made
her way to a vacant table in the far corner and settled
facing the room. A friendly waitress brought her a glass
of shandy. Sarah and Tod were already established with
drinks at a table beside the door and Foxy was waiting
in the van, around the nearest corner. Foxy had Alice's
mobile phone and Sarah had its number in her pocket

along with change for the payphones in the hall. There was nobody else present who could possibly have called himself an 'old friend'.

Alice waited. She had not been there before. The bareness of the room was relieved by prints of old maps, framed and hung on the walls. She would have like to wander round and look at them, but it seemed more politic to remain where she was.

A figure showed palely in the darkness outside the big windows and Alice thought that she was being observed. A figure – she thought the same figure – showed a minute later, watching through the glass doors from the hallway. A little later the young man entered, gave a searching glance around the room and then headed for her table.

Alice registered the fact that the appearances of Tod and Sarah seemed to mean nothing to him. By the time he towered over her she had recognized his face, connected it with the voice on the phone and even managed to recall a name from the past.

'Well, well, well,' she said. 'Justin Dennison. And now you're an old friend, suddenly.'

He produced a wry version of a smile which she had once thought attractive. 'I like to think so. After all, we danced together a few times and went on a couple of dates.' He sat down and waved away the hovering waitress.

'One date,' Alice said firmly. 'Which ended abruptly when you grabbed hold of me and planted a kiss on me which nearly turned me inside out.'

His smile became reminiscent. 'All right. Blame me if it makes you feel better. I apologize. Perhaps I was young and impetuous and I didn't realize how virginal you were in those days.'

He was a nice-looking young man in a slim and

intellectual style, with brown hair which sometimes rose uncontrollably and at other times flopped lankly over his eyes, varying its texture, Alice had thought, with his moods. He was neatly dressed in a leather jacket, flannel trousers and well-polished shoes, but she noticed dog or cat hairs on his jacket and his tie was slightly off-centre. There was a thin line of stubble where his razor had missed. She recalled that she had wondered, at the time, whether her reaction to the kiss might not have been unduly resentful or would have been different if he had approached her a little more circumspectly. But that seemed to be a subject best avoided for the moment. 'What happened to you after that?' she asked. 'You seemed to drop out of sight.'

'I went to London to do a course and serve an apprenticeship. But I'm back now. How did you come to be a burglar?'

'I didn't.'

He looked her squarely in the eye. His hair was definitely in its buoyant mode. 'You diverted the police with bogus alarm calls while your pals cut their way into the strongroom at the supermarket.'

'Then think of me, if you must, as a sort of telephonist.' She decided to draw a bow at a venture. 'And now you're recording this conversation. What are you? Police?'

He seemed to be genuinely amazed at her comment. His hair seemed to settle down. He opened his soft leather jacket to show the whole of his thin shirt. 'Good God, no! If it eases your mind, I'll say aloud that all I'm after is a share of the take. So, if there was a tape – which there isn't – that would make it entrapment and therefore almost certainly inadmissible in a court of law.'

Neither the gesture nor the argument was conclusive but his manner was convincing. All the same, she decided to be cautious. 'The money is probably shared out and a long way away by now.'

'I don't believe that it's gone beyond recall. And, anyway, I'm not talking about the supermarket's money. Twenty-three grand, shared around four or five? Peanuts. It's the euros I'm talking about.'

So the unpleasant Mr Farquhar had bumped up the loss for insurance purposes, either to cover his losses from shoplifting or to make room for a little bonus to himself. She needed a little time to think; and thought was difficult while he was probing her with eyes which she had once thought sympathetic. She wondered whether her face was betraying her.

'Excuse me for a moment,' she said. She tapped her empty half-pint tumbler. 'I need a pee.' And before he could protest, she stood up and walked towards the door. He half rose as she left the table. The old-fashioned gesture was somehow reassuring. She winked at Tod and Sarah as she passed them. Reflected in the glass doors, she could see that Justin had made no attempt to follow her.

The toilets were off a short passage leading to a side door onto the car park. To reach the Ladies, she had to pass the reception desk. That put a much-needed thought into her mind, but she continued into the toilet and washed her hands while cogitating furiously. When she came out, she stopped at the reception desk and looked in their Yellow Pages.

She arrived back at the table hiding a complacent smile. Justin got up again until she was seated. Even during discussions of criminal conspiracy, good manners prevailed. She liked that. Looking closely at his hands, she saw that although they had been scrubbed and the nails cleaned with care there were signs of staining and the calluses of work between his fingers.

'Suppose I tell you to go and bowl your hoop?' she said.

'Suppose I go to the police?'

'You can't. You're the engraver. I remembered that you were going in for something artistic. I just looked in the Yellow Pages under Engravers and there you were in your own name. You came back from London and opened your own little workshop.'

His face and hair showed that she had hit home. 'I could tip them off anonymously.'

'And you think that I wouldn't mention your name? The police would only have to search your workshop.'

He raised his chin, looking defiant. 'My workshop's had the spring clean to end all spring cleans. Some prat got caught trying to take some of the euros abroad. He's kept his mouth shut, but they knew the area he came from and as the nearest engraver I was immediately suspect, but I'd seen it coming. They had forensic scientists crawling all over my workshop and they couldn't find a thing.' He laughed shortly. 'All right. So we're each as bad as the other. I was struggling to keep afloat while I waited for business and I was tempted, but all I got for engraving those plates was a none-too-large flat fee while I was handing them, almost literally, a licence to print money. I still want to get something extra for myself out of it. So what now?'

'Until this moment,' Alice said slowly, 'I had only one channel back to the . . . the organizers. Mr Farquhar.'

'And a useless creature he is,' said Justin. 'I don't believe he even knows what's in the boxes. He just rents out space in his strongroom.'

'And now we've got you. The question is, are you any more use than he is?'

'That depends what you want.'

'I expect it does.' The advantage of using a go-between known to the forgers was obvious. The potential disadvantage, that Justin knew her identity, was offset by the fact that he didn't know where to find her. Alice's mind was racing ahead. She had no chance to consult the others without risking letting this chance slip through her fingers. Go for it, girl, she told herself. 'I see it this way,' she said. 'We haven't counted the euros but on the basis of a little sampling I guess that there are about three million euros, say two million pounds. Whoever goes around passing the notes is taking most of the risk, so I suppose – guessing again – that half a million pounds would find their way back to the forgers. Of course, they could start printing again. Perhaps they have cupboards full of euros all over the place. But it would still be worth their while to buy them back from us for a tenth of what they expect to get for them. Say fifty thousand genuine pounds up front. If you can set up that deal, you'd be in for a sixth – a bit over eight thousand.'

He sat and thought about it, eyes half closed, while a faint smile came and went. She felt a passing impulse to lean across and straighten his tie. 'And if I can't?' he said at last.

'If you can't, then I certainly can't. In that event, we may market them ourselves on the Continent. Or they may wake up some morning to find that a trail of counterfeit euros leads from the doorstep of the police station to the supermarket and from there to the print shop and the paper-works. You can tell them that. And there's one condition. You do not under any circumstances tell them who I am.'

'That's reasonable. And you don't tell your pals who I am?'

'Agreed,' Alice said. 'And, while I think of it, what put you on to me?'

His smile emerged all the way. 'No harm telling you, I suppose. It was the purest chance. I'd been competing in a darts match at the Strathlinnie Inn which went on until after the usual closing time and then I hung about talking with friends. I was walking home. It's a long walk and my feet were tired but the taxis were all taken. I saw you go into the phone box and recognized you. I had never forgotten. You have . . . a piquant face. And the sexiest walk there ever was, which is what rang a bell with me. The nearest seat was across the road and some yards along. I sat there, meaning to speak to you when you came out, maybe to share your taxi if that's what you were phoning for.' He paused and produced another and warmer smile which lit something inside her. 'I planned to make my belated apology and show you that I'm not always so impetuous. As my eyes got used to the darkness, I could make you out. You kept looking at your watch. Then you made another phone call and another. You only keyed three digits each time and I never saw you put any money in the box, which meant the emergency services. Then you came out in a hurry and a car picked you up. I didn't think anything of it until I read about the robbery. The papers said that the police received a spate of bogus phone calls. It was as simple as that.'

'Simple, but it still required intelligence!' Alice said. 'Perhaps it's just as well, if you can pull it off. If they ask you how we got in touch, what are you going to tell them?'

'What's wrong with the truth?'

Alice had been warming to him. She had wondered how to get him back onto the subject of her attractions. After all, he was a nice-looking young man who had once shown a fancy for her and was to be pressed into useful service; but if he was going to think through cotton wool he would be no use to her. 'If you tell them that, you'll have to tell them who I am,' she pointed out.

'True.' He half-closed his eyes again. After ten seconds, they opened again. 'How's this? I knew that somebody had been hanging around my workshop a few weeks ago but I assumed that they were watching the bookie's office next door. Then I arrived at work one morning and found that the lock had been forced. Nothing had been taken and the plates were already gone, but the intruders had broken open the cupboard which the plates had been kept in. The cupboard backs onto the wall of the bookie's office so I assumed that they had been prospecting to see what the chances were of breaking through that way.'

'Did you tell the police?'

'Would I want to draw the attention of the police to my workshop? But it must have been somebody after the plates, so my connection with the euros was known; and this morning I got a phone call insisting that I act as an intermediary. I'm going to meet somebody in an hour's time.'

Alice nodded approvingly. He was a fluent liar. He had recovered in her estimation. They would make a good team. 'When you've got a reaction, call me on my mobile.' She glanced at her plain, digital watch. Now that she was in funds, she really must buy something a little more ladylike. 'I think that I should be going.'

He jumped to his feet. 'I'll walk out with you. That's natural enough, one-time boyfriend and girlfriend.'

She blew her nose, leaning back to be sure that she was in Tod's line of sight. Then she got up and took his arm. As they passed Tod and Sarah, Alice winked.

They left by the side door and paused in the darkness

outside. 'I think your figures were a serious underestimate. I might push for more than fifty grand,' he whispered.

'But don't kill the deal by being greedy.'

'No.' He changed position. 'And, now that I've apologized for being precipitate last time, I think that I should try again, but more gently this time around, first pausing to mention that I've always thought you the most desirable girl in Britain, and charismatic with it.'

Alice had a new and enlightened attitude to the mating game. 'No harm in trying, I suppose,' she said. 'I'm a bigger girl now.'

The kiss began as a respectful brushing of lips but, when Justin found that he was not being repulsed, it progressed rapidly through friendship to passion and turned at last into mutual bear-hugs and a twining of tongues. He smelt of talcum powder and tasted of peppermints. The old Alice would have been repelled by such unhygienic though erotic intimacy, but not the new.

He broke away suddenly. 'I'll be in touch,' he said. He walked quickly away across the grass towards an estate car several years old. Alice made her way on wobbling legs towards the van. Tod had never affected her like this.

Chapter Nine

A lice waited until they were back at the cottage before giving more than the baldest outline of the story. Then she gave the others almost a word by word account of her meeting with Justin Dennison, only playing down mention of their past and present relationships. These she preferred to keep to herself for the moment. Tod's reaction might be uncertain and she would have disliked being teased while her own feelings were in turmoil. In retrospect, it now seemed obvious to her that her earlier reaction had been seriously immature while her sudden attraction to him would make her look, to Tod at least, like a fickle and immoral jade.

It proved surprisingly difficult to fulfil her promise and keep Justin's identity from her companions. Having admitted that she knew who he was, that he had been a participant in the forgeries and that he was to be the go-between in selling the euros back to the forgers, she found herself pressed to reveal more.

'I don't see what harm it would do,' Sarah said petulantly, 'at least to tell us what his function was. I mean, we've got to put a lot of trust in him and all we know is that he's a former boyfriend of yours who recognized you at the phone box and put two and two together.'

'He promised to keep my identity from his bosses,' Alice pointed out, not for the first time, 'and in return

I promised to keep his identity from you. I can see his point. Anybody can let something slip, or try to strike a deal with the police if the whatsit hits the fan. I don't know about you but I keep my promises. We can trust him, and that's that.'

It was not a satisfactory answer, but imperceptibly Alice had drifted into the position of leader. Sarah, whose antennae were ever alert for any hint of romantic entanglement, had seemed quite unaware of any attraction between Tod and Alice but was intensely curious about what had gone on between Alice and Justin in the past and whether the spark still glowed. Reluctantly, the others accepted Alice's edict; but the suggestion of distrust left a tension in the air while they frittered away the next two days. When another walk along the beach was proposed, she declined to recognize a strong hint from Tod that they should both remain for an hour or two of dalliance. Tod left in a huff for the beach-walk but Alice was pleased to remain alone and potter instead with some minor domestic chores.

She was relaxing with a cup of coffee, made just as she liked it with a touch of chicory, sugar and a drop of cream, when her mobile phone played its little tune. She had been awaiting, with some impatience, a call from Justin, so she was not surprised when his voice came on the line.

'At long last,' she said. 'I've been waiting to hear from you.'

'Longing to hear my dulcet voice, I hope,' he replied, 'rather than anxious about business.'

'Both.'

'Oh well. Fifty-fifty isn't a bad average. I haven't been able to get hold of the big cheese yet but I'm seeing him later today. I'd rather not say too much on the phone. I wondered if you'd meet me at the Cameron Arms again and I'll give you an update.'

'I could do that. Sevenish?'

'Great. Stay for dinner, my treat. And, Alice, I've been recalling more and more how attractive I found you and how well we were getting on before I went and spoiled it by rushing in. And I think that you remembered something too.' He paused. 'I have a feeling that I'm not speaking to deaf ears.'

Alice felt an inner glow but she kept her voice cool. 'Nobody has ever accused me of being deaf.'

'Don't think that I'm pressuring you – I'd hate to spoil things again by rushing them, but we're both older and wiser now. I was also wondering whether I should book a room. What do you think? I'm very, very keen but I leave it up to you.'

Alice's first impulse was to retreat indignantly from such a provocative invitation. But a later withdrawal would still be possible and when she conjured up a memory of that kiss she found that the pressure of his lips, the slither of his tongue, the clean smell of him and the feel of his hardening body were fresh in her mind. She felt her breath quicken.

'You could do that,' she said. 'Booking a room wouldn't cost very much. You can judge for yourself whether you're going to be able to afford to waste that sort of sum.'

'I quite understand,' he said, and Alice was sure that he did. There was a warmth and satisfaction in his voice before he rang off, suggesting he was already sure that the room would not be wasted.

With nearly eight hours to idle away, Alice would have had time to spring clean the cottage and still make her preparations several times over. But all other distractions were driven out of her mind by an emotion that she could only think of as eagerness. She told herself that she was in danger of becoming a slut, but the pleasurable thought of her mother's disapproval was enough to tip the balance the other way. She hurried through her self-imposed tasks, pumped water up into the cistern and then took a leisurely shower, perfumed herself and dressed from the skin out in her best and finest. She took time over her hair and makeup. If she bestowed what remained of her virtue on Justin, he was to be given no grounds for complaint.

When the others returned, dropping into chairs while they emptied the sand from their shoes, Alice's obviously sunny mood overrode the lingering tension.

'Best bib and tucker?' Sarah exclaimed. 'What's the occasion?'

'I don't call it an occasion. I've had a phone call at last,' Alice said. 'He's seeing the boss-man this afternoon and I'm to meet him this evening to get the news – at the Cameron Arms again.'

'It's an occasion all right,' said Sarah. 'I bet you've got glamour pants on.'

Alice retained her dignity and kept her skirt out of Sarah's reach. 'I'll be having dinner with him, so can I borrow the van?'

'No problem,' Foxy said. 'Just be sure you don't run out of fuel.'

It was time to let her secret out. 'I may be staying overnight.'

The others sat up. Tod looked put out and Sarah triumphant. 'That's a bit quick, isn't it?' Foxy said.

'I knew him ages ago.'

'Hah!' Sarah said. 'Knew him? In the biblical sense? And I thought you were – you know!'

Alice avoided Tod's eye. 'What I was and am and have done and will be doing this evening is no concern of yours,' she said cheerfully. 'And I'm doing no cooking in this dress, so you can worry it out between you.'

'You can give me all the details later,' Sarah agreed.

'Just a minute!' Foxy said. 'We may want the van before you two have finished with each other. I wouldn't mind going for a beer.'

'One of you can drive me there and bring the van back,' Alice suggested. 'I'll leave you my phone and then, if he tells me I've got to walk home, I can call and tell you when I want to be picked up.'

'He won't do that,' said Sarah. 'He looked too much of a gent and much too smitten. I'll go with you. I'd like get another look at this charmer. He must really have something.'

'I'll come along for the ride and treat myself to a beer before we come back,' Foxy said.

'All right,' said Sarah. 'But only one. I wouldn't want to share a jumbo jet with you when you've been on the beer, let alone a van. You can buy me a gin-and-something. Coming, Tod?'

Tod, whose nose was definitely out of joint, said that he preferred to stay in the cottage and relax with the radio for company.

'We'll get a bar meal and Tod can look after himself,' Foxy said happily.

Foxy preferred to drive. He had found a new interest in his van now that its exterior had been refurbished and he was spending his spare moments cleaning out the dirt of years and chasing and silencing rattles, with the result that he now treated other drivers with all the mistrust to be expected of the fond owner in possession of a new Ferrari. Alice took the passenger seat and Sarah rode in the back.

They left in good time, drove through an evening which contrived to be damp without actual rain and arrived at the Cameron Arms with some minutes to spare. The car park was half full. Alice was feeling a little chilly about the feet and she was reluctant to expose herself too openly to general view. She was having difficulty dividing her concentration between her adventure into the arms of Eros and the exchange of money for the return of the euros. She directed Foxy round the corner of the building to the shaded and almost empty leg of the L-shaped car park. He reversed into a place in the shadows near the side door.

There was a dark estate car parked further along to their right which looked very much like Justin's. Perhaps, in his eagerness, he had arrived early. But Alice had been imagining herself in the position of the gang responsible for the forging of the euros and she could see that this was definitely a danger moment.

'Give me a minute,' she said. 'I want to see that everything's OK.'

She slipped out of the van and went in through the side door. The lady at Reception, sniffing disapprovingly, confirmed that Mr Dennison had booked a room by phone but that he had not yet claimed the room key. Alice wended her way around each of the interconnecting bars, braving some audible masculine attention. There was no sign of Justin. She returned to the van.

Sarah had moved into the passenger seat. Alice spoke through the open window beside her. 'I'm not a happy bunny,' she said. 'He booked a room but he hasn't shown up yet, although I remember him as a compulsively punctual person. And that looks very like his car there. Colour me uneasy. I have a touch of the premonitions.'

'It could be imagination running away with you,' Sarah suggested.

Foxy stirred and smacked his lips. 'While the two of you argue it out,' he said, 'I'll go inside. If you need me, I'll be in the public bar.'

'Wait,' Alice said.

As she spoke, another car swept into the car park and headlights swept across the other vehicles in that quiet corner. For a moment the other car and a pale van beyond it were brightly lit. 'I'm damn sure something's wrong,' Alice said softly. 'I'm sure that's his car, but there are two men sitting in it, waiting for something. I was sure he'd be alone.'

'I'll tell you something else,' Sarah whispered. 'While the lights were there, I saw something silhouetted in the back. It moved, that's why I noticed it. I thought it was a dog's tail at first but then I decided that it looked like a hand. I think there's someone lying across the back seat.'

Alice felt cold fingers up her spine. 'I like this less and less,' she said. 'I want to take a look. If they're quite innocent, there'll be no harm done. Foxy, if Sarah draws one of the men off, could we cope with the other one?'

'I'm joco,' Foxy said. 'Anything less than a gorilla with a chainsaw, I can cope.'

'You're a tough little bastard, aren't you? Why do I have to be the goat?' Sarah asked.

'Because you always could run faster than I could and you've got trousers and trainers on. This skirt's a bit tight for sprinting and I have the wrong shoes. Foxy, you realize that there could be two men to deal with, if the man in the back isn't who I think it is?'

Foxy humphed. 'Dig the jack-handle out of my box and leave it to me.'

'All right. But don't kill anybody.'

'I'll try not.'

Alice's plans were soon laid. They waited while a people-carrier arrived and a group of six entered the hotel. Then the car park was quiet again. Sarah dismounted and walked towards the estate car, peering towards the back. When she was still several yards off, there was a sudden movement and Sarah turned and bolted towards the side door of the hotel. She pretended to trip and went on, limping more slowly. The temptation was enough. A man erupted out of the driver's side of the car and lumbered in pursuit. Sarah recovered suddenly. As soon as both were out of sight in the hotel, Foxy started the van, put up his lights and jerked forward in a neat semicircle, stopping nose to nose with the estate car.

Alice had sprinted beside the van. Leaving it to Foxy to look after the other man, who was already half out of the passenger's door, she ran to the rear of the car. By the reflected glare of the van's lights she saw a figure curled on the back seats. With difficulty, she recognized Justin. Blood on his face looked black in the reflected light. He moved, weakly. Ignoring the sound of strife from the other side of the car, she jerked the door open. Justin seemed barely able to move himself. In the emergency, thought became instantaneous. Moving him might worsen some serious injuries but the delay in calling for an ambulance and skilled paramedics would almost certainly entail an exchange of violence and the attention of the police. Flight and leaving him to the mercy of his assailants was not to be contemplated.

Justin would have to take his chance. Alice took him under the arms and pulled. He yelped and came out of the car like a sack of potatoes. He still had some use of his legs, which suggested that no major bones were broken, but he hissed with pain. She helped and hustled him, stumbling, to the back of the van, opened the door and rolled him inside, following in a single leap just as Foxy piled into the driver's seat.

The van backed hastily away and Alice saw that a man was lying against the side of the car, holding his head. Whether he was still moving, she had no time to see. They were nearing the front door of the hotel. Sarah came out in a hurry. Foxy checked the van and Sarah ran round and threw herself into the passenger seat. Her pursuer, who had followed her on a brisk tour through the bars, had presumably been inhibited from overhauling her in the hotel foyer and was running a poor second, but the check gave him time to arrive at the offside front door of the van. It was his bad luck that Foxy had managed to drive without losing hold of his jack-handle. Alice heard a muffled whack.

Seconds later, they were out of the car park and on the open road. Any disturbance beyond the opening and closing of car doors seemed to have gone unnoticed, or if there was any alarm among the foyer staff they were leaving it far behind.

'Nobody following us?'

Foxy looked in the mirror. 'One bus, half a mile back.'

'Is he all right?' Sarah asked.

'I wish I knew,' Alice said. Swallowing her anxiety, she leaned down and addressed the figure sprawled at her feet. 'Are you all right?' she asked. The only answer was a low groan. 'I'll take that as a no,' she said. She took hold of his hand. 'Just hang on.'

There would be little to be gained and much to be lost by attempting first aid at the roadside and any such attempt would have been impossible in the moving van. Alice was determined to avoid doctors and hospitals unless and until proved absolutely essential. Her resolve, however, began to falter when Justin's grip on her hand weakened and became limp. She switched on the interior light without more than a token protest from Foxy. Justin's face was barely recognizable, swollen and stained with blood. His pulse, however, seemed adequate and he was breathing steadily, so she switched off the light and concentrated on trying to stop him rolling around on the floor of the van while she thought out her next moves and, when they arrived at last at the track, demanding that Foxy try to pick his way between the potholes.

Foxy was exasperated. 'If you think you could do better, change places and drive.'

'I'm tempted, but I'm needed back here.'

Alice's emotions, if she had taken the time to analyse them, were mixed. Along with concern for Justin and anxiety to hear his story in full was indignation that the blossoming of the new Alice, the swashbuckling rebel against the world, was to be thwarted by enemy action.

When the van stopped at last, she flung open the rear door and dashed into the cottage. Tod had inflated the airbed and was taking his ease on it but she turfed him off with the absolute minimum of explanation. It took only a few seconds to move a few of the boxes of euros so that the stack more nearly resembled a low altar for human sacrifice. Anxiety and impatience had given her extra strength. With the old counterpane replaced, the stack began to look suitable for a sick-bed. Only then did she return to the van. Foxy and Sarah were hovering uncertainly over Justin. She cajoled them into carrying Justin very carefully into the light.

It was already obvious that Justin had been subjected to a considerable beating. His face was swollen and discoloured and the bruising extended to much of his body. There was a swelling the size and shape of a fried egg on the side of his head, but Alice was relieved to see that the blood on his face seemed to have come from a common nosebleed. He had lapsed into unconsciousness but Foxy, who seemed to have some knowledge of first aid, rolled up his eyelids one at a time and expressed an opinion that Justin would not enjoy waking up but he would awake. A gentle exploration by touch suggested that if any of Justin's ribs were cracked, at least none of the fractures was displaced. They undressed him carefully, fed him dispersible aspirin and covered him with the spare blankets.

'We'll leave him to sleep it off,' Alice said. She found an empty coffee jar and washed it out. 'This is for if he feels sick. You're quite sure nobody followed us?'

'Absolutely,' Foxy said. 'No question. If anybody followed us they were invisible, or in a helicopter.'

'All right. We'll check him again and get his story in the morning. Meanwhile . . . it may seem a little callous, but I didn't get the dinner I was promised. How about it, Sarah?'

'I'm just as hungry, but you may as well do the cooking,' Sarah said. 'That isn't your best dress any more. You've got blood down the front.'

Alice looked down and groaned. 'You cook,' she said. 'I must sponge this dress.'

Tod, who had earlier thrown together a scratch meal for himself, denied being hungry so the three sat down late to a mixed grill. Alice, in one of the communal dressing gowns, ate while keeping one eye and an ear on Justin, but his breathing was regular and Foxy was adamant that the patient had passed into natural sleep and should be left alone.

'This is all very well,' Tod said glumly, 'but you've given him my bed. Where do I sleep tonight?'

'We can manage with the two chairs,' said Foxy. 'Then we'll be ready with the aspirin and the coffee jar whenever he wakes.'

'My hero,' said Alice.

Justin did wake in the night and groaned pitifully. Alice got out of bed, but Foxy was already busy with aspirin and a cold compress and Justin managed to pee into the empty coffee jar and lapse back into sleep without speaking. His urine was examined critically but contained no blood.

Justin was still sleeping when the four, who had been late to bed and disturbed in the night, awoke at last. The sound of breakfast dishes roused him and he groaned again. Alice got up from the table and helped him to sip a cup of tea.

He looked at Alice through eyes which would barely open between swellings like purple sausagemeat. 'They beat the shit out of me,' he said huskily, 'but I didn't tell them who you were.'

'You're sure?'

'Fairly sure. I said that I was there to meet a girlfriend who had nothing to do with any of it. I don't know if they believed me.'

'They won't believe you now,' Alice said.

'I suppose not.' Justin licked dry lips. Alice could see that his eyes were still unfocused. 'More tea?'

She supported his head again and held the cup for him. 'Better,' he said.

Foxy, standing over him, recovered from an enormous yawn. 'Neither of those neds will be feeling much better than you are.'

'You're sure you didn't kill either of them?' Alice asked.

'Don't think so. I gave the first one a knee in the balls,' Foxy remarked casually, 'and then punched him up the throat. I hit the other one with the jack-handle, but I only got him across the nose and mouth. He'll be spitting out teeth for a week.'

'That makes me feel better,' Justin said. He dozed off again.

The four moved outside. The day proved fine and almost warm.

'I don't like this one damn bit,' Tod said. 'They'd rather play rough than pay up. I'm going to take my two grand and bugger off.'

'I'm with you,' said Foxy.

'You're a fine pair,' Sarah sneered. 'The first hint of trouble and you're over the hills and far away.'

'It's all right for you two,' Tod pointed out. 'You haven't done anything except make a few phone calls which they've no way of connecting to you and which they'd have a hell of a job proving. All you've got to do is walk out of here and shut the door.' He saw that Sarah was on the point of explosion and hurried to qualify his remarks. 'I don't mean that you haven't pulled your weight, just that you haven't stepped much outside the law.'

'Well, I'm going to stay here and look after the . . . the patient,' Alice said.

'I'll stay,' said Sarah, 'at least until I've heard the rest of what he has to tell us. Before you take the van away, shall we do what Alice said and lay a paper-chase from the cop-shop to the supermarket?'

'You're joking,' Foxy said. 'Aren't you?'

'God, you are thick sometimes!' Sarah said. 'It's time we went in and woke him up again.'

Justin's eyes were open when they gathered around his improvised bed.

'How do you feel now?' Alice asked.

'Bloody awful. But not quite so bloody awful as before.' His voice was hardly more than a whisper but his eyes could now focus.

'Are you hungry?'

Justin considered. 'Couldn't chew anything. More tea, perhaps? Or soup?'

'I'll make it,' Sarah said. 'Do you have any broken bones?'

Justin stirred, moving his limbs cautiously. He coughed. His voice was stronger. 'Don't think so. Not too sure about my ribs but they don't hurt much if I keep still and don't cough. Those men seemed careful not to do permanent damage, as if they were afraid of consequences or thought they might want to use me again. I've still got my teeth, though one of them's loose.'

'You'd better tell us all about it,' Alice said. 'Is your memory functioning?'

'It's a bit patchy and I can't be sure what's real.' For the first time, he looked around the simple room of the cottage. 'Where am I and how did I get here?'

'We brought you here in the van,' Alice said. 'Don't you remember? This is where we've been staying.'

Justin seemed to have been drifting along in a passive state, waiting for the normal world to return in its own time, but now for the first time he showed signs of agitation. 'Is Humph here?'

'Not unless you call one of us Humph.'

'Humph's my dog. He'll be worried and hungry and he's probably made a mess. Where's my car?'

'We left it back at the Cameron Arms. You were as much as we could cope with. It's probably still there.'

Justin tried to sit up but groaned and lay back again. 'Let me think. The money's hidden in it.'

'*What?*'

'You got the money?' Alice exclaimed.

'I think so. I've had some weird dreams but I'm sure I didn't dream that. I saw the boss-man.' Justin's voice was getting stronger. 'I told him I'd found that my workshop had been entered and that was how somebody'd known to get in touch with me – the story as I told it to you, Alice. I said that you wanted sixty grand and I repeated your threat about the paper-chase. I said that you wanted an immediate deal.

'I expected that he'd need time to raise the money, but he left me sitting for half an hour and came back with an attaché case full of used notes. I guess they've been passing fake euros on the Continent already, that's how so much cash was on hand. I said that I'd relay instructions about where to pick up the boxes of euros. I was surprised they were so trusting, but it's obvious now that they never meant me to get clear with their money; they just wanted to be sure that I'd make a bee-line to you and the euros.' He sighed, winced and sipped from the tea that Sarah was holding for him. 'I was going to pour the notes over you, Alice, in . . . our room and let you wallow in money.'

'A romantic! They'll have grabbed the money back by now,' Foxy said.

'Don't think so. Unless you've owned one of that model, you probably don't know that there's a compartment under the floor at the back, under the boot-liner. It's awkward to get at, so even owners usually forget that it's there. Those two sods, in between knocking me about and wanting to know who you are, searched the car. Then they punched me some more and asked where the money was and I kept telling them that I'd already delivered it. They didn't believe me, though I'd been in and out of several shops and spoken to a dozen people, so I suppose I'd been followed. I thought

I'd been too careful for that. Please, go and look after my dog.'

'Is he savage?' Sarah asked.

'He's a soft lump. He'd give any intruder a nasty lick. Please . . .'

'The car will be gone by now,' Tod said.

'For sixty grand, it's worth taking a look,' said Foxy. The others were standing around Justin but Foxy had stretched out in one of the easy chairs and he spoke without opening his eyes.

'Let me think,' Alice said.

Sarah gave the patient a drink of soup. The others waited patiently while Alice thought. She found that she was developing a knack for operational planning.

'This is how I see it,' she said at last. 'Foxy says we weren't followed—'

'I'm positive.'

'—don't interrupt – and they've no link to Gordon, so they can't possibly know where we are. They'd need a lot of people to pass the notes when the time's ripe, but those wouldn't be part of the counterfeiting organization. That wouldn't need many people and I wouldn't expect them to have many strong-arm fellows on the strength. Justin?'

'If I knew they had any,' Justin croaked, 'I wouldn't have agreed to be your messenger. Please, will somebody go and look after my dog?'

'Maybe they only had the two and those are both laid up for the moment. But let's assume that they're still capable of operating in the field. We need a distraction.

'They'll have searched your home, Justin, but they won't have found anything. I think we wait until midafternoon – if we go now, we'll get there around lunch-time and the Cameron Arms will be so busy that we won't be able to tell if anyone's lurking. Around the time we get started, Justin phones the boss-man and says that he just wants out and the euros can be collected from some remote place. I suggest the derelict barn you took us to on that first evening, Tod, where Foxy went back to spray the van. It's just the right distance. They can't afford not to go and look. So that should draw off some if not all of their remaining manpower. We approach cautiously and aim to bring the van and the car back here.'

'Sounds OK so far,' Tod said.

Sarah nodded. Foxy merely snored.

'Let him sleep,' Alice said. 'He was awake for most of the night. I'm only thinking aloud. Sarah, we'll leave you to look after both of the sleeping beauties. Now, what Tod and I do when we get to the Cameron Arms depends on whether Justin's car's still there. If it's gone, we can report it stolen. If the . . . the opposition haven't found the money, the police won't give a recovered car that much of a search. But if the car's still there it all depends on whether it's being watched and, if so, whether somebody's actually sitting in it. So here are three versions. Plan A goes like this . . .'

Chapter Ten

After a snack lunch and leaving Alice's phone with Sarah, who was spooning soup tenderly into Justin, Tod and Alice set off in the van.

'You're getting keen on this young bloke, are you?' he asked as he drove.

'Yes. Do you mind?'

'I've no call to mind. I hope he's good to you. You'll always be special to me.' She could tell that he was depressed.

Justin's address turned out to belong to a small house in a quiet street of small houses, built around the time of World War One and now mellowed and weathered and cloaked in the green of creepers and small trees so that the street was the very picture of comfortable cosiness. It was a street where Alice could imagine Justin being happy, and his companion too. The narrow street was already cluttered with parked cars but there was a space for the van. Almost opposite Justin's house was a small park.

They walked back two houses. 'I'll come in with you,' Tod said.

Alice nodded. 'Somebody might be lurking.'

She had Justin's house key on a ring with his spare car key, but it proved superfluous. The door had been forced and pulled shut again so that the damage to the woodwork around the lock was inconspicuous. Alice summoned up her courage and pushed at the door.

They were greeted by a tempest of barking. A large golden retriever was in the hall and prepared to defend it against a second intrusion. Tod hesitated on the doorstep but Alice, more accustomed to the ways of dogs, put on a show of friendly confidence and offered the back of her hand. The barking subsided into a deep growl which set the hairs crawling up the back of her neck, but it was enough for her that the big tail was moving gently. Alice was ready to snatch her hand away if threat turned to attack, but managed not to let her fear show in body language. An old-fashioned hall-stand loomed beside her and among the coats she saw a leather-and-chain dog lead. Moving slowly, she took it down.

As she had hoped, the person holding the lead represented authority and walks. The dog had been shut in for at least twenty-four hours and that need must be paramount. She attached the lead to a now puzzled but complacent dog. 'Take a look around,' she said to Tod.

'Right. What am I looking for? The money can't be here.'

'I know that. Look for dog food and his dish.'

The dog – Humph – almost pulled her off her feet. He was in no doubt as to where they were going. He had a slight limp and Alice wondered whether it was a long-standing complaint. She was led firmly across the street and along fifty yards of pavement to the park. There, Humph stopped expectantly. It was a nothing sort of day, neither warm nor cold, not dry without being quite wet, almost but not quite calm, heavily overcast, but he seemed glad to be out in it. Keeping one eye out for hostile park-keepers, Alice let him off his lead and the big dog vanished into the nearest shrubbery. He emerged again after a minute and set off in a heavy gallop around the grass before returning to Alice and nosing her hand. The message was clear. They returned to the house.

In looking around, Tod had left doors open and the signs of a thorough search were unmistakable. Furniture had been tossed around and upholstery slit. They could at least have let the poor damn dog out for a minute, Alice thought, into the neat back garden which she could see through the window of a small, outdated kitchen. She would have liked to begin restoring order, but time would soon be pressing. Tod had found a large bag of dried all-in-one dog food in a cupboard and a stainless-steel bowl beside the sink. She put food in to soak. While Humph tucked into what Alice, scaling up from a Labrador's needs, estimated to be an appropriate meal, she took her own look.

The house was in the process of being turned into a personalized home. The sitting room and hall had been redecorated in bright, contemporary colours while the rest of the house was still drab and old fashioned. Some new furniture had been brought in but the rest, Alice guessed, had been legacies from a family home. Most of it was ruined and she hoped that Justin was insured. Books and CDs had been scattered during the search. Justin had a taste for modern novels and non-fiction but nothing too ponderous. His taste in music was for lighter classics and there was also a strong representation of traditional jazz – which latter went to explain the dog's name. Well, it could have been worse – Dizzy, perhaps, or Satchmo. Alice found herself understanding and empathizing with Justin even more than before. He was not just a sexual magnet, he was her sort of person.

Humph had finished his meal and taken a drink of

water. He should be walked again but time was pressing; he could wait until they reached the cottage.

Alice used Justin's phone to call her own mobile number. She reassured Justin as to Humph's well-being. No, he said, Humph had not been limping. One of the bastards must have kicked him. She hung up and waited while Justin made the planned phone call about the euros and he called back to report that it had been received without thanks or comment. It was time to go. Alice put the lead on Humph again.

'Nice little place,' Tod said. 'I could just do with a house like this. You're bringing that monster with us?'

'It could be ages before Justin's able to look after him.'

'I hope he isn't another one wanting a slice of the cake,' Tod said. 'He'll smell the place out.'

'No worse than Foxy,' Alice said.

'Foxy's a lot better, thanks to you.'

'So you owe me,' Alice said.

They pulled the door to as neatly as they could. The damage was invisible from halfway along the path. No neighbour seemed to be at home to pay any attention. It was a neighbourhood where people kept themselves to themselves. Humph, who had accepted Alice as a friend, entered the van without demur.

They had timed it well. The Cameron Arms was open but it was wrapped in the calm that comes over hotels in midafternoon, even on Saturdays. There were a mere half-dozen cars, evidently empty, scattered about the car park and the only people in sight were a couple hurrying towards a white Land Rover. Justin's estate car was still where she had seen it last.

'Go,' she said. 'Plan A.'

132

'Right.'

Tod drove round the back of the hotel and parked against the wall near the bins outside the kitchen door. Alice gave Humph a pat and told him to stay where he was. She crossed the tarmac and entered the conifers which half-circled the car park. Darkness was coming in early under the overcast, in the fading light the trees cast deep shade and the going was difficult. The ground was uneven and in places was encumbered with undergrowth, some dead but some very much alive. Brambles tore at her legs and, as another pair went the way of all tights, Alice was sorry that she was wearing a skirt and blouse instead of her more usual jeans and a sweater. She groped and stumbled her way, as quietly as she could manage. Tod would be watching from the corner of the hotel, ready to gallop to the rescue if the car was a trap.

She kept well back from Justin's car so that any watcher at the edge of the trees would show up in silhouette. All seemed well. She studied the outline of each tree but nothing moved or protruded, so she took a closer look and then, stepping out onto tarmac, peered into the car. It was unoccupied. She dropped into the driver's seat, found the ignition slot and, groping with the unfamiliar controls, nearly stalled, headed for a corner of the hotel, was saved by the power steering and finally drove off, finding the light switch at the second attempt. The indicators proved to be on what seemed to her the wrong side. The radio was playing softly but she had no attention to spare for it. In the mirror she saw the van pull out and turn the other way. Her mouth was bone-dry. She still had only a learner's licence, but that was a comparatively minor crime to add to the rest.

Two miles up the road and the car had begun to seem familiar. But there was another car in her mirror. She recognised the twinned headlamps of a BMW. It could have been perfectly innocent but on the other hand it could have been waiting, concealed among cars parked outside nearby houses. There was a large and confusing housing estate on her left but Alice had been friendly with several girls who lived there. She turned and cruised carefully around the twisting streets, emerging onto the main road through a different junction. No other vehicle seemed to be on her tail. She set off again in the general direction of the cottage. There was a short shower which left droplets to refract oncoming lights all over the windscreen. A cyclist barely escaped with his life before she found the wiper switch again.

Outside the town, other traffic was thin but there was enough of it to make recognition of a particular vehicle difficult. She pulled into a bus layby and parked. She felt safe with a queue of would-be passengers beside her. Three BMWs went by, or perhaps the same one more than once, before a bus arrived and forced her to drive on.

Was she being followed? There was one way to find out. She turned into a B-road which connected two major arteries. After a minute there were lights behind her, too far off to distinguish the car. She speeded up, emerged onto a dual carriageway and put her foot down, carving through the slower traffic with all the confidence which is the prerogative of the inexperienced.

She came off onto an A-road and in another ten minutes was approaching the track to the cottage. But she did not feel safe. A car had been coming up behind her and she was almost sure that she could make out BMW-type headlamps. She passed the track and made a turn in the opposite direction from the cottage, towards a small town which she had visited often. A car turned to follow, but she could not be sure . . . She slowed right down but the car behind came no nearer.

Houses showed up, their lights reflected in the newly wetted road. She drove through a brightly lit square, turned by a church and again immediately beside the school. Round the back, all was darkness except for a bright moon emerging from the overcast. She found the path she wanted, switched off her lights and set off diagonally across the playing fields, swerving to avoid a sudden set of goalposts. The going was soft. The groundkeepers would bless her in the morning.

At the furthest corner, lights on again and a gateway let her out into a quiet street of houses which curved down to a bridge over a narrow river. Up the other side, round a mini-roundabout and back across the bridge, no car lights moving. She left the town by a different road, still heading in the general direction of the cottage.

The radio was still playing, distracting her. The music was her least favourite pops. She gave Justin the benefit of the doubt and assumed that his assailants had also retuned his radio. The volume seemed to have increased. She fumbled for an on-off control. She must have changed the waveband or a tuner. The music was replaced by a steady, repetitive electronic signal.

'Shit!' Swearing had never come habitually to her and she bit the word off. Her neck clenched as she took in the implications, and her stomach was uneasy.

The road she was on came out not far from the track to the cottage. She had told Tod to drive around for long enough to be sure that he too had shaken off any pursuit. Sod's Law suggested that he had already given up and made for the cottage. But . . .

She neared the end of the track and hesitated. There was a vehicle coming the other way, larger than a car, smaller than a truck. She went to main beam for a few seconds. The other vehicle also undipped in angry response but she had time to see two tones which looked very like those of Foxy's van. She fumbled and sprayed the windscreen. Wrong side! She changed hands and flashed repeatedly. The van slowed and stopped.

The road was blessedly empty. She braked, jerked the car viciously round and completed her turn on the grass verge to park behind and beside the van. Tod jumped out to meet her. 'Listen to this,' she said. 'I think they've planted some kind of homing bug in the car. And I think I've seen the same car half a dozen times, a BMW, not very new.'

Tod listened to the chirping radio for a few seconds. He thought quickly. He turned and grabbed one of the lamps out of the van. He opened the back of the estate car, pushed aside a rug and an old coat and raised the plastic boot-liner. A section of floor was easily lifted. Beneath was an attaché case. It was not locked. Tod lifted the lid and they saw money neatly held by rubber bands.

A car was coming, blazing light at them. Tod dropped the boot-liner and the lids. They froze. But the car swept past and away.

'That wasn't them,' Alice said.

Tod opened up again and lifted out the attaché case. 'It was a Rover,' he said. 'Leave the car here and get in the van. Quick.'

The car was safe enough on the grass verge. Alice grabbed the keys, killed the engine and lights and locked the car. Tod was already in the van with the case beside him. Alice jumped in and took the case on her knees. Humph greeted her with relief, snuffling at her neck. She stroked his big head.

Tod had the van moving before she could close the

door. 'Where would they get a gadget like that in this neck of the woods?' he asked.

'Out of a lifejacket, probably. I expect the lifeboat was launched before anyone realized that the signal was coming from somewhere inland.'

Tod turned into the track. He tried to drive without lights but soon the shadow of trees made this impossible. 'How long do you reckon we've got?' he asked.

The van was bucking over the potholes. Alice tried to think while desperately hanging onto the door handle. 'Don't know,' she said. 'If they know where I've been, they can probably figure out that my manoeuvres were centred around somewhere near here. The car isn't far from the mouth of the track. In their shoes, I'd give it a try, sooner or later. But if there's one bloke on his own in that car, they may have to gather their forces. It might depend whether they have radios or mobile phones with them.'

'They'd be mad to come out on a caper like this and not have them,' Tod said.

The track had twisted towards the moon and Tod was driving without lights again. Quietly, Alice opened the attaché case, felt for the neat packets of notes and began transferring them through the neck of her blouse. They settled above her waistband where she hoped they would not be too conspicuous under her coat. She was not overly busty but, on the other hand, she had not, in her mother's idiom, 'been hiding behind the door when bosoms were handed out'. She closed the latches as they skidded to a halt before the cottage. Tod grabbed the case out of her hands as she got out of the van and shook it. He seemed to be reassured by the weight remaining inside.

Humph followed Alice heavily out of the van, pausing to relieve himself against one of the wheels. In the otherwise vacant room, Justin seemed to be in an uneasy sleep. His bruises had swollen and progressed from blue to a greenish purple. Humph put his great front paws up on the boxes and sniffed Justin's face but he seemed to realize that his master was best left in peace and he settled at the foot of the boxes with his eyes anxiously raised. Alice passed them both by for the moment. There was no doubt in her mind that they would have to go while the going was good and she wanted her possessions with her.

In the bedroom, she was confronted by a singular spectacle. Clothing was scattered across the floor. Foxy and Sarah were on the bed, conjoined and moving with an accelerating rhythm. Sarah was on top, presenting her bare bottom to the beholder.

It was too much. Frustration and nervous tension had brought Alice to an emotional pitch and now an irrational fury was added to the rest. How dare they achieve the release which she and Justin had been denied? And, the final insult, they were doing it on her side of the bed! The blood pounded in her ears and her rage exploded. She stepped forward and swung her arm with all her strength, delivering three huge slaps across that bare bottom. Then she waited, nursing her stinging hand.

There was no immediate reaction to the violence. Clearly passion had reached its climax. Foxy was emitting a series of groans while Sarah had thrown her head back and was giggling insanely. Their convulsions became frantic. Alice's three overlapping hand-prints went from pink to scarlet.

Alice shrugged and began stuffing clothes from the wardrobe into her bag with shaking hands. Facing away from the bed, she loosened her blouse and let the money fall among the clothing.

The two on the bed disengaged. Foxy, modestly keeping his back turned, shuffled out of the bedroom. Sarah rolled over, stretched and blinked at Alice. 'Did you wallop me across the bum?' she asked.

'I did. We've got a crisis.'

'You'll have to come and do it again next time. It was brilliant. One thing added to the other.' She paused and looked blankly at Alice. 'What crisis?'

'There was a homing bug planted in the car. They'll find this place eventually, without a doubt. We'll have to move.'

'I heard that,' Foxy said from the door. He had got as far as putting on his trousers.

Alice carried her bag out. Justin was awake and peering at her through his swollen eyes. Humph was up on his hind legs, his head on Justin's chest, whimpering with joy at his master's caress and his tail sweeping the air. 'I heard it too,' Justin said.

'Could you make it in the van with us?' Alice asked him.

Justin pushed Humph's head aside and tried to sit up. He collapsed with a groan. 'Don't think so. I'll stay. They've already thumped me, they've no call to do it again.'

Alice was looking further ahead. 'Is there anything in your workshop to connect you with the forgeries?'

'Nothing. I made damn sure of that after the plates were finished and delivered.'

Alice looked round the others. Sarah, wearing a dress and probably nothing else, had the cocoa jar in her hands and was pulling at the packed bundle of notes. Tod was groping under the sink. Foxy, still bare to the waist, re-entered, nursing a bundle of sand-dusted notes and a cut finger.

Alice decided to stay. There might be something that

she could do for Justin. 'You go,' she said. She took Justin's hand and received a squeeze in return.

Tod was undecided. 'We'd probably meet them in the track,' he said.

Alice decided that she was tired of doing everybody's thinking for them. Perhaps one more time . . . 'Drive along the beach,' she said. 'The tide's out and the sand should be firm enough where it's still damp. You can manage without lights under this moon and the incoming tide will wash out your tyre tracks. Go as far as the rocks. There's another track to the road from where the burn comes out, but if you wait around there I may try to join you later. If not, give me a phone some time.'

Her advice seemed to be accepted without question. Panic had infected the others but not to the extent of leaving their hard-won fortunes behind. Foxy, with his shirt hanging out and one arm out of his sweater, leaped into the van. Tod, moving jerkily, heaved two boxes of euros out of the stack, almost displacing Justin, and tossed them into the back of the van. Possessions were hurled on top.

'Lights entering the track,' Sarah squealed.

That was enough. The three leaped for the van. Alice followed them out.

If the balance of the sixty thousand was waiting for them, the fury of the gang of forgers would be considerably abated. 'Leave the attaché case with me,' Alice said. She made a grab.

Tod's eyes were staring. He had been caught up in the panic of the moment. 'No way,' he said. 'We've got to have it.' He gave Alice a push which was almost a punch, so that she staggered back and, tripping over a tussock, sprawled on the sandy grass. The van lurched away, heading on a light throttle towards the beach.

*   *   *

Alice picked herself up. The sandy ground was surprisingly hard, but although she had twisted her leg slightly she was otherwise unhurt. She shook her fist at the departing van. Tod's had been a definitely unfriendly act, she decided, from one who had been her lover once – but only once and he had since been on the point of being supplanted. Some day, perhaps, she would have a chance to pay him back – indeed, she had a suspicion that the time might be coming uncomfortably close. Or had he been acting out of frustration and jealousy? But no. There had been no love. She shied away from putting a name to what there had been between them, but love was definitely not the word.

She glanced once towards the track. The glow of lights could be seen above the trees. She limped quickly into the cottage.

'Stay where you are,' she told Justin. 'I can't do any good here for the moment and I might make things worse. I'll come back as soon as it's safe. You should be all right.' She touched his cheek gently. 'You can take the credit for recovering most of the euros on their behalf despite the way they treated you. Play your cards right and they may even end up feeling that they owe you something.'

He grabbed for her hand. 'But you will come back?'

'Of course I'll come back. If I can't make it back while you're still here, I'll find you at home. Remember, we snatched you out of your car because we wanted to know about the money but you refused to tell us. Tell them that the money's still in your car.'

'Can't. I told them I'd already taken it out.'

Alice was running out of time. 'Then Tod and Foxy grabbed it off you. Improvise something. If it'll save you any more grief, just mention my name. You do understand?'

'They'll know that I lied to them.'

'You could have believed it at the time.'

'Yes. You're right. There's nothing you could do here. You're better away. Take Humph with you. I don't want him kicked again or worse. Go, go, go.'

She bent and planted a kiss on his lips. Even at such a moment, the magic was still to be felt. Humph pushed jealously between them, so she snapped the lead onto his collar before grabbing up her bag and bolting through the door. Humph paused on the threshold and looked uncertainly back. His weight and strength were too much for her to drag but, seeing no sign from his master, he relented and came along.

The van was out of sight but the oncoming lights were almost clear of the trees.

The spade was where Foxy had thrown it down. The night was turning very frosty and the spade was freezing cold, cold enough to burn her hands, but her gloves were buried somewhere in her bag. At the rear corner of the cottage she threw her bag aside and, still holding the lead, dug in the spade one-handed. The ground resisted and then gave way, but it took her several heart-stopping seconds to find her tin of money. She hesitated and by then it was too late, vehicle lights were playing across the front of the cottage and spreading over the rough ground to either side. Should she wait in the shadows and hope that nobody looked around the back? But they would have to be impossibly casual not to check for a possible ambush. She leaned against the back of the cottage and tucked the money from the can into her bag. There must be quite a useful sum in there by now and she was not going to abandon it without a struggle.

There were voices from the front, more than one. Three she guessed, but there might have been more. Lights came on in the cottage and the vehicle lights died. She heard footsteps sounding hollow on the floor and the voices became muffled. It was time to go. It was now or never. She began to run but was jerked to a halt by Humph's weight. He looked at her, uncomprehending. She wanted to shout at him, but that would be fatal. She patted her thigh in the universal gesture, coaxed him into a walk and then a canter. She ran, limping slightly, with the big dog loping beside her, for the nearest fringe of forestry. Her footsteps made only a grating sound on the sandy earth and, thankfully, Humph had decided not to bark, but the chain of the lead jingled whenever she let it go slack. The slight upward slope and the softer ground made for heavy running and her dark clothing, which might render her invisible against the dark trees, must be conspicuous against the moonlight on pale grass and sandy soil.

She was fifty paces short of the trees when a man's voice, no longer muffled by the fabric of the cottage, was raised. She had been seen, she knew it. Nothing to do but to flee onward. If she could only shake off pursuit she might be able to hide her bag and circle round. There might still be something she could do for Justin.

She reached the trees and plunged between, forcing her way with branches tearing at her clothes and larch and spruce needles going down her neck. The trees had been planted ridge-and-furrow and had been left to grow until the branches had begun to mingle. The resultant tangle was hell to push through and, at the same time, noisy, while Humph seemed determined to seek an easier path on the other side of each tree. Alice got down and crawled, using two knees and one hand, with the lead and her bag clenched in the other hand. Three or four rows in from the edge, she turned towards the track. The going was easier deep in the furrows and the ground was soft and relatively quiet, but hauling her bag was a complication. Why oh why had vanity impelled her to dress up instead of wearing her customary jeans and sweater? To tow the bag and the dog behind her required a hand which she needed for crawling and Humph kept walking onto her legs.

When Humph jerked the lead out of her hand and crashed deeper into the trees, she was almost relieved. She sat up carefully, removed the belt from her coat and anchored the bag to one of the loops. Only innate stubbornness made her persist . . . that, and having, for the first time in her life, some money that she could, with a slight stretch of the imagination, call her own.

She heard her pursuer. Only one man, she thought. He tried to force his way in among the trees but he must soon have realized that the going would be slow and noisy. Through the stems of the trees she could make out his figure, moving almost parallel to her. Then she lost sight of him. Humph seemed to be pushing his way in the opposite direction, towards the beach. Given a little luck, the man had made a bad guess and turned the other way, following the sound of the dog. It might have been a reasonable assumption. The beach was nearer and would be an easy avenue for flight. But Justin's car was near the mouth of the track and she still had the key. She could wait for the visitors to leave and go back for Justin. Or, if they took him with them, she could follow. But how would she know? Or if the car was gone or disabled, she had – she checked her pocket – she still had her mobile phone. She could call a taxi. She could afford the fare for once. She tried to clear her mind.

She struggled on. It would be a long haul. She had lost track of the man and God alone knew where Humph had got to. The night was silent. She could have made better progress with a breeze to rustle the branches and cover her sounds. Her knees and elbows were becoming painful. A haze had come over the moon. If she could not see her pursuer, perhaps he could not see her.

A sound alerted her, the jingle of the chain. She could make out a shape beyond the edge of the trees. That was all she needed. Humph, the great stupid, adorable mutton-head, out of misguided devotion for his new friend, had come looking for her. He was romping along, tail going, enjoying a game of hide and seek, pausing now and again to sniff at what might have been a rabbit hole. She lay still. He would neither see nor hear her, but a dog depended more on its sense of smell. Was she emitting a cloud of scent – pheromones? – to betray her? When she looked again, he had vanished.

Perhaps it would be safe to emerge and walk close to the trees. She covered another ten yards while she considered. But no. Caution above all and Humph was still out there, looking for her. Life became an endless endurance. One elbow and the opposite knee, then change sides. The hand which had slapped Sarah's bottom was stinging. A startled woodpigeon clattered out of the trees overhead, betraying her position if her pursuer had any understanding of the countryside. She tried to think about something other than her miseries, to remember the plot of a film or mentally recite a poem. The pain became less if she tried not to think about it. If she could ignore it altogether, perhaps it would go away. Had Justin tried that? What was happening to him, back at the cottage? She had been cold but now, with all the exercise and in the shelter of the trees, she was uncomfortably hot.

After an age of misery, the light seemed to change. The moon had cleared, but it was more than that. Suddenly she realized that she was seeing the moonlight on the track and the first phase of her misery was almost over. She knelt up carefully and undid her belt. The bag could wait here until it was safe. Perhaps she should do the same. She transferred a few packets of banknotes and a handful of loose money to her pocket in case of future need, closed the bag again and waited.

A week earlier, she would certainly have called the emergency services; but, for the moment, she had no desire to have the police asking questions. To cause a distraction, she could have used her mobile to call for an ambulance, but the police would certainly be notified if a badly beaten-up man were collected from a remote cottage. Who else might she call? Her father? She shivered at the thought. Perhaps she should phone every taxi operator for twenty miles around and order each of them to send one cab to the cottage. In the confusion . . . But, in the confusion, anything could happen. The unpredictable never figured in her plans.

She had been a long time among the trees. Would she have heard them if they had collected the boxes and departed? She was cold again, bitterly cold. A lady, her mother had told her, never sweated, but there was certainly a dampness of perspiration drawing out the warmth from her body. The leg which she had twisted was paining her.

This last was the decider. If she stayed crouching beneath the branches for much longer she might not be able to walk away at all. Leaving her bag behind, she crawled to the end of the trees and rose cautiously to her feet at the side of the track. Which way to go? While she thought about it, she began to replace her belt.

Her moves had been anticipated. A dark and heavy figure detached itself from the trees beside her and took hold of her arm.

Alice was exhausted from the long crawl and her leg had

stiffened to the point at which she could not have run. The grip on her arm suggested that her captor was very strong. There seemed little point, therefore, in struggling. After one convulsive leap, she stood still.

'You come along,' said the man. His voice was gruff and locally accented.

He set off towards the cottage, but immediately Alice's stiffened leg let her down. She stumbled and nearly fell, but the man took it for an attempt to escape. He swung her round, pushed her to the ground and knelt, straddling her back and squeezing the air out of her. He took the still dangling belt out of her hands and used it to strap her wrists together, too tightly, behind her back. Then he picked her up over his shoulder in a fireman's lift and started off again along the track.

It was the most miserable journey of Alice's life. She would happily have exchanged it for another crawl between the trees. The belt around her wrists was painfully tight. Her breasts were now bruised, completing the inventory of pains throughout her body. Screaming would have been a waste of breath – even if she had had some to spare, because her weight was fully on her stomach and to breathe at all was a major challenge. Blood was rushing to her head. Her captor was making very free with his hands, but that was now the least of her sufferings. All that she could see was her own dangling hair, a broad back and sturdy legs and the rough surface of the track receding in the moonlight. The changing shadows and the sound of surf gave her some measure of their progress and, whatever awaited her at the cottage, it had to be preferable to this torment.

Chapter Eleven

A lice could only be sure of their arrival at the cottage when she glimpsed part of a dark car and the man clumped up the two steps, rapping her head against the doorpost. Then she found herself dumped into one of the kitchen chairs. During the seconds that it took her to recover her breath, the man produced a sheath knife and cut two lengths of rope from the coil on the cottage wall. He circled her waist, arms and the chairback twice with the longer piece, pulled it tight with all his considerable strength and knotted it. Breathing became difficult again but it was possible. The shorter piece he used to tie her ankles to the bar of the chair.

Justin, she saw, had been rolled onto his face and his hands and feet were tied. He caught her eye. Among the bruises she recognized a look of desperation but he made a gesture of clamping his lips firmly shut and she understood the message.

For the first time, she got a good look at her captor. He was large. He had a big belly but she already knew that the fat overlaid a great deal of muscle. His black hair was lank and greasy. Above a bulbous nose pitted with large pores, his prominent brow ridges and shaggy eyebrows shaded a narrowed pair of eyes.

Another man was sitting opposite her at the kitchen table. He was of a leaner build. His head had been shaved

148

although a dark stubble was growing back. His hands, she noticed, were ingrained with a dark stain and his nails were black. He was nursing a mobile phone while his eyes feasted openly on those parts of Alice which a gentleman only studies surreptitiously. 'You brought me a present? My birthday's not until tomorrow,' he said.

'You're at the back of the queue,' the fat man retorted. 'What did the heid-bummer say?'

'He's coming out with a van. He should be well on the way by now. We'd never have shifted this lot in a motor.'

'So we wait. If he says to get rid of these two . . .' He stooped and his hand strayed across the front of Alice's dress.

It was too much. Justin's message had been *least said, soonest mended* and she had been thoroughly in agreement, but now her only weapons were words and she only wished that she had not led the sheltered life which had resulted in such an impoverished vocabulary. Larding her speech with the few swear words under her command, she called him a dirty animal, the son of a long line of child-molesters and a sweaty, poncy pig who would wipe his bum on his mother's face if he'd run out of handkerchiefs. She also called him a wanker although she had only the vaguest idea what the word meant. Drawing comfort from the only attack available to her, she progressed onward into still wilder flights of the imagination.

The fat man showed little reaction. His sneer suggested that he had been called worse. He left the cottage and returned with a length of Duck tape which he plastered across Alice's mouth, cutting off her invective. She could only seethe, between trying to exchange telepathic messages with Justin. Her predicament was beyond logic.

She was seated, more or less hale, in a familiar chair, but because of a piece of tape and some bits of rope she could neither move nor speak. She willed herself to stand up and walk, but her body was unable to respond. She had become a parcel.

The other man had been listening with a broad grin. When Alice's invective was cut off, he said, 'She's got you to a T, Pug. If she gives that description to the police, they'll have you in cuffs within minutes.' His voice was surprisingly educated, coming from one of disreputable appearance. The combination was intimidating.

'No names, you daft docus,' the fat man said. 'She's not getting as far as any cops.' He flicked Justin contemptuously. 'As for you . . .'

'What did you expect me to do?' Justin asked weakly. 'I bloody *told* you I'd handed over the money. I went on to meet my girlfriend and you grabbed me and beat me up. When they got me out of there, of course I went along with them. My chances were better with them than with you.'

'Fucking liar,' Pug said. He gave Justin another flick which made his head jerk. 'How do you explain that phone call you made, eh? And if this isn't your girlfriend, how come you fetched up back here?'

'We had a date. This is where we were going to meet.'

A third man paused in the doorway and looked at Alice. He had a wild mop of curly hair around a bald crown. His appearance triggered Alice's memory. His had been the figure on the ground after Foxy's attack. 'Very decorative,' he said. 'There's naebody else out there, but I see tyre tracks on the sand. Your friends left you behind, sweetheart. And I have a pal who's looking forward to meeting you again. Your driver owes him some teeth.'

150

Behind his back, Humph looked cautiously in at the door. Intervention by a large, soft-mouthed and woolly-minded dog could do nothing but harm. Alice could only shake her head at him. She never knew what, if any, message he had received but his face vanished again.

The skinhead had got up from his chair to look in the cupboards and find the slender store of drinks.

'Better stick to beer,' said the fat man. 'The boss-man would hit the roof if he found us getting pissed. Put the hard stuff in the boot of the car and we'll have it on the way home.'

The beer was shared around. The third man went to the door to keep watch, but his vigil only lasted a few minutes before a vehicle could be heard labouring over the rough ground and pulling up outside. All three went out. Alice struggled with her bonds. If she could only get free, she could surely do something, find some weapon. But the knots were well out of reach and her fingers were going to sleep. She tried to stand up and shuffle to the kitchen cabinets where there would be a choice of knives, but the rope at her ankles defeated her. She bent her neck, trying to rub her face against her shoulder to move the tape, but with her arms pulled back and jammed between her body and the chairback it was impossible. It was cold with the door open, or perhaps it was just the chill of fear.

'Bring the boxes out,' said a different voice, more educated and authoritative than any of them. 'I'll check them off.'

The three men returned. Justin was lifted ungently to the floor and the men began to carry out the boxes of euros. Alice was smitten with new panic. Surely the boss-man would not drive off without even looking inside the cottage, leaving Justin and her to the mercy of his minions. She began to jerk herself forward, trying desperately to move the chair towards the door.

The fat man, Pug, lifted the last of the boxes and grinned at her. 'Don't you worry, darling,' he said. 'I'll be back.'

'Two missing,' said the boss-man's voice. 'It could be worse, but we'll take the change out of somebody's hide.'

Alice, who had moved a few inches at the expense of her wrists and ankles, gave up and resorted to a loud humming sound through her nose.

A burly figure, topped by a face with a Roman nose and full lips, appeared in the doorway, followed by the other three men. She was suddenly aware of her state, dirty with her clothes ripped and her hair like a gorse bush. The newcomer exclaimed. He stepped forward and ripped away the tape.

'I caught her just before she made it along the track,' Pug said.

The newcomer sighed. 'It would have been better if you'd let her get away.' He stooped and twitched her skirt down towards her knees.

Alice had been storing up a thousand things to scream at them as soon as the tape was off, but all of a sudden her fear and fury were turned upside down. She moistened her stinging lips. 'Hello, Dad,' she said.

Her father looked at her through narrowed eyes. 'Have you been spying on me?'

'Never,' said Alice emphatically.

'Then what the hell are you doing here?'

'Waiting for you to untie me,' Alice said. 'It was pure chance. We didn't even know about any euros.'

He shook his head and gave a brief chuckle. 'So you

were one of the gang who robbed the supermarket. You! If I'd known that you had that much get-up-and-go I might have recruited you myself.' He paused thoughtfully. 'But probably not. I set your life in motion and now I feel responsible. I wouldn't want you to follow too closely in my footsteps.' He chuckled again. He seemed to be in a rare good mood. 'A prime case of "Don't do as I do, do as I say".'

'And if I'd known that you were the mastermind behind the forgers,' Alice said, 'we'd have done some other supermarket. To think that I sat there and let you pontificate to me about becoming a useful citizen and not sucking from the public tit! Untie me.'

Her father's face clouded over. He shook his finger under her nose but he seemed to be having difficulty formulating a satisfactory and unanswerable retort.

He was presented with another and more urgent subject for his concern. The skinhead bolted through the door. 'Men sneaking up on us.'

Alice's father stepped to the window. 'Who?'

His question was answered from outside. The cottage was suddenly bathed in light and an amplified voice was raised. 'This is the police. You are surrounded by armed officers. Come out, throw down any weapons and raise your hands.' The message was repeated.

His three henchmen began to swear but Mr Dunwoodie kept his head and thought furiously. For the first time in years, Alice felt a bond with her father. It must have been from his genes that she had inherited the knack of calm thought in an emergency. He shook his head suddenly, leaned forward and replaced the tape, which he was still holding, over Alice's mouth. 'You're better where you are,' he said. He ruffled her hair, a gesture which she had hated as a child but which had become strangely comforting, and stepped to the door, putting up his hands in the universal gesture of surrender.

Alice was once again reduced to the position of a passive parcel, unable to do anything but listen. Justin seemed to be inert, receiving none of the telepathic messages which she was firing at him in rapid succession.

From among the voices outside, one took over – a resonant voice full of the confidence of authority. 'Well, well! Robin Dunwoodie Esquire,' it said cheerfully. 'I have great pleasure in taking you into custody. I may as well tell you now that you've been under observation for several weeks. We've been holding our hands, waiting to find you in physical contact with the forged euros, and until now you've been too careful. This time, you've slipped up. You are well and truly nicked.'

'I have no idea what you're talking about,' said her father's voice. 'I only came out to collect some bits of fishing tackle from my cottage and I found these men removing some boxes—'

'A good story,' said the voice, 'and one which might have stood up if we hadn't spent the last ten minutes videotaping by infrared while you helped stack the boxes in the back of the van which you had personally driven here. And now I must warn you that anything you say will be taken down and may be used in evidence. Before formal interview, I shall also warn you that any facts you intend to rely on in your defence should be produced immediately or they may be discounted by the court. And now, let's see what we still have inside.'

Alice's father, his hands behind his back, reappeared. He was followed by a thickset man in a heavy overcoat and a tweed cheese-cutter cap. 'Well, well, well,' said the latter. 'More of the gang?'

Alice's father stood very still. 'Do they look like

members of the gang?' he enquired tiredly. He sighed and took a deep breath. 'This is my daughter. She knew nothing about any of it. When I learned that she had gone out here I realized that she would find the boxes and might even fall foul of my men. They wouldn't know her from Eve and might have been rough with her, so I came out in a hurry to tidy up and clear the cottage. I was too late. I never meant her to see me but I suppose she was bound to find out eventually that I wasn't the pillar of virtue she's always thought me.' He met her eye and gave her a secret wink. 'Don't think too badly of me, child.'

Alice tried to smile at him, if only with her eyes.

Outside the cottage there seemed to be much activity, but Alice, once she and Justin had been cut free, was kept waiting within. Police vehicles arrived and later, after her father and his three minions were driven away, an ambulance arrived for Justin. Alice wanted time to think before having to explain herself to the senior officer (who turned out to be a Detective Chief Inspector Cowiesson). For that reason, as much as because of her concern for Justin, she insisted on accompanying him to the hospital. The DCI, perhaps in a hurry to interrogate his prisoners, surprised her by allowing it. Her tender conscience had supposed that she would be interrogated and possibly locked up.

A moment's thought satisfied Alice that there should be no incriminating material in Justin's car. 'My boyfriend's car is still at the main road,' she said.

'You could drive it.'

'I only have a provisional licence. If one of your officers could sit with me . . .'

DCI Cowiesson let it be seen that he wanted nothing more than to be rid of Alice, at least for the moment.

155

'That is not what they're for. I'll have it driven to the police pound.'

'Thank you.' No doubt the DCI's helpfulness was encouraged by the opportunity to search the car, but there was no harm in being polite.

Alice's only other words to the DCI had been, 'You won't get much help from my boyfriend. His memory's very patchy.' By one quick glance, Justin managed to indicate that the message had been received and understood.

The paramedics tutted over Justin's injuries and lifted him gently onto a stretcher. They also anointed Alice with a lotion which greatly relieved the rope-burns on her bruised wrists and ankles and the soreness of her lips. They were accompanied in the ambulance by a plain-clothes woman detective who sat on a jump-seat with a notebook inconspicuously on her knee, but if the DCI was hoping that she would record some revealing conversation he was doomed to disappointment. After winning her small battle with Mr Cowiesson, Alice had gone on to argue with the paramedics that Humph, who had appeared again out of the darkness now that all the angry words had finished, could not be abandoned miles from anywhere. Humph was allowed to join them in the ambulance on Alice's assurance that he had no parasites and had full control of his bladder.

They travelled with Justin's hand resting in Humph's coat. Alice gripped his other hand as far as the Infirmary, where they were gently but firmly detached. She would, in any case, not have been allowed to take Humph inside. She was told to go home, on condition that she attended at the police station for interview before noon the next day.

This left Alice with no option but to be delivered by Panda car to the parental home. Humph was grudgingly accepted into the car but only on condition that he squeezed in somehow beside Alice's feet. Men in blue uniforms, Alice decided, lived in fear of getting yellow hairs on themselves.

By now, the hour was late and Alice's mother was already in her dressing gown. She had received news of her husband's arrest and, although perturbed, did not seem surprised. Alice's brother, Ronald, was also present to lend moral support and legal advice but soon left to attend, in his capacity as a solicitor, his father's interrogation. Alice gathered that Mr Dunwoodie's activities had not been totally unknown to his wife, but the subject was carefully avoided between them. Mrs Dunwoodie was mildly curious about Alice's activities during her absence from home but accepted a repetition of the story about 'staying with friends' without showing open disbelief and seemed more concerned over the state of her clothing and the unexpected addition of a second and larger dog to the household. However, Suzy, the family Labrador, seemed pleased to have canine company for once and, after a suspicious sniff or two, the two dogs settled down amicably in the single but generous dog-nest, curled together into a surprisingly small ball.

Her brother, similarly, while offering her support and his services as solicitor, had accepted without comment her bland statement that she was innocent of all wrong-doing. When he was leaving, he had a quick word with her in the hall. 'I saw Dad for a minute or two and I'll go back when they interview him in the morning. He seemed remarkably cheerful when I saw him, considering the pickle he's in. I gather that he made a pretty damning admission.'

'He did, though I think his position was already hope-less,' Alice said shortly. Her father's words had been weighing heavily on her. There could be no doubt that he had thrown away his chance, however slim, of bluffing it out in order to give her a chance to exonerate herself.

'He gave me a message for you. I don't know what it means and I don't want to know, but he said, "Tell her not to try to spend any of that money." Does that make sense?'

It made perfect sense to Alice. The money in the attaché case was as counterfeit as the euros. Too bad! 'I'll puzzle it out,' she said. She would have preferred to try out versions of her story on her brother and was aware that keeping one's lawyer in the dark could be a quick road to trouble, but she had an uncomfortable belief that, as a sworn upholder of the law, her brother might be unable to support her in any story which he knew to be untrue.

By morning, after a restless night, she had thought out her options. She dressed quickly, reverting to jeans and a hideous jumper (a Christmas present from an aunt which she found at the bottom of her wardrobe). She had had enough good clothes ruined for the moment and decided to conserve what remained and, anyway, her better clothes were still in her bag nestling among the trees. Her mother and her brother had left to visit her father in the remand centre, so she had exclusive use of the telephone. The day being Sunday, she found Gordon Watkins at home. Without preamble she said, 'Gordon, the shit is in process of hitting the fan. You're in the clear for the moment and I'll keep you out of it if you'll do one thing for me.'

Over the phone, she heard him swallow anxiously. 'What's that?'

'Just remember, if the police ask you, that I spent Friday night with you and yesterday you drove me where I wanted to go.' She described exactly where Justin's car had been left. 'Can you remember all that?'

'I can remember.' Gordon had made a quick recovery. 'I could remember better if the first part was going to become true.'

'Not in your wildest dreams. Just bear in mind that if somebody dropped a hint about where the Stihlsaw came from that was used in the supermarket robbery, you could go down the drain along with the rest.'

Gordon was hurt. 'You don't have to be like that. I just hoped that you'd be properly grateful.'

'I shall be grateful,' Alice said, 'but not that damn grateful. And, remember, under no circumstances do you admit having made any phone calls. And don't let them get your voice on tape. As it is, they may think of comparing my voiceprint with the tape of the emergency calls.'

'Now just a holy minute!' Gordon's voice went squeaky with nerves. 'If I'm seen to be an associate of yours, they may go after my voiceprint.'

She admitted to herself that he had a point. 'Then suggest somebody else who could back up my story.'

There was silence on the line until Gordon said suddenly, 'I have a friend. He'd do anything for a couple of hundred.'

'Is he respectable enough to be believed? Does he have a police record? Is he gay?'

'Yes, no and no.'

'I suppose he'll have to do. I'd better meet with him, straight away if not sooner.'

Gordon called back within minutes. Alice brushed the needles off her coat and took the two dogs for a walk along the rough of the golf course. Paul Henson was waiting in the shelter beside the fifth tee. They sat inside, out of the chill breeze, just another young couple. Alice looked him over carefully. He seemed tidy and good-looking enough to make a credible lover. She waited while a mixed foursome drove off and then explained exactly what she wanted.

'I could do that,' he said. 'But Gordon said that there'd be a couple of hundred in it for me. I'm behind with the payments on my car, and if they repossess it I'll lose what I've already paid.'

'You don't have to explain. I can give you two hundred in real money,' Alice told him, 'but I have eleven hundred in good forgeries, take your pick.'

'Let's have a look at them.' He studied several notes carefully, comparing them with a note from his wallet, before making up his mind. 'I know somebody who'll buy these off me,' he said. 'It's a deal.'

Despite her relief at unloading her father's forged pounds and retaining her share of the supermarket money, it was Alice's turn to be cautious. 'I don't want you getting into trouble and losing your credibility,' she said. 'You're sure he's to be trusted?'

'He's my cousin.'

That was not necessarily a full warranty but it would have to do. Alice waited while a male foursome arrived. One of the men came over to make a fuss of the dogs. When they had driven off, she said, 'All right, then.' She handed over the wad of notes and saw them vanish into a deep inner pocket. 'If there are any repercussions, I've never heard of that money. Now, the police may never check up on my story but, just in case, describe your house or flat to me and then we'll agree exactly what happened.'

When she got back to the house, her mother and brother had returned. Her brother drove her to the police station in his new Rover.

Nearly an hour later, they were escorted into an interview room where they were joined, after another wait, by

DCI Cowiesson accompanied by a uniformed constable. A tape-recorder was turning quietly on a side table and there was an indicator light on a video camera. Now that she had a chance to observe him in less fevered circumstances, Alice noted that the DCI was a cheerful-looking man with hollow cheeks and thinning hair.

'My brother is also my solicitor,' Alice said. The DCI raised an eyebrow, so she added, 'Yes. I feel the need for my solicitor. Your first words on seeing me were "More of the gang".'

The DCI looked mildly amused. 'I see. Then let's get down to business. How did you come to be at the cottage last night?'

Alice put on her most frank and honest look for the benefit of the video camera and was careful to avoid any of the customary signs of prevarication. She found that she could still think clearly while a part of her mind was telling her to speak at her usual speed and not to still the small movements of her hands and body. 'I had arranged for my usual boyfriend to meet me at my father's cottage on Friday evening.'

'Why?'

Alice's laugh was genuine. 'Really, Chief Inspector, if you were to have a rendezvous with me at a remote cottage at night, what would you think we had in mind? Anyway, I told him that I'd promised to attend a hen party and that I'd try to get out of it, but I might not be able to make it that evening. I told him to make himself at home and I'd come when I could. Just in case my father turned up, I told him to leave his car on the main road and walk along the track.'

'What was the point of that?'

'So that he could slip away and I could pretend that I was there on my own. Really, Chief Inspector, you don't seem to have had much experience in secret love affairs.'

The constable looked amused but the Chief Inspector, who until then had avoided showing any expression at all, pursed his lips. 'I haven't,' he said. 'And where was the hen party?'

Alice simulated a look of coy frankness and looked at her brother. 'Ron, you're here as my solicitor, not as a member of the family. That was just a story, Chief Inspector. I had another date with a different friend. I really didn't expect it to go further than a good meal and a lift out to the cottage, but he turned out to be great company. I spent the night with him and he gave me a lift to the end of the track the next day, yesterday, in the afternoon. There was a van outside the cottage, but I only thought that a meter-reader had turned up, or some workman sent by my father to fix something. But there were three men there and a lot of boxes and they'd been beating up my boyfriend. I tried to run. I got into the trees, which is why I was in such a state when you arrived, but they grabbed me and tied me up and one of them went outside to use a mobile phone. And that's really all I know.'

The constable was hiding a grin but Ronald and the Chief Inspector both looked slightly shocked. 'Mr Dennison's injuries looked older than that,' said the DCI.

'Older than what? I don't know when they started laying into him and when those men left us alone for a minute I spoke to him, but he didn't seem to remember anything.'

'Your mouth was taped.'

'That came later. I thought that they must have done some permanent damage to his brain and I told them what I thought of them. They didn't like it much.'

'And when did your father arrive on the scene?'

'You know that better than I do.'

'I still want to hear it from you.'

'If you insist,' Alice said with great patience. 'He arrived only minutes before you did.'

'How many minutes?'

'Really, Chief Inspector,' Alice said indignantly, 'I wasn't watching the time. I'd been roughly handled and tied up and I couldn't see my watch. I didn't know who was coming. I was afraid. It seemed soon. I wasn't counting the minutes.'

'You could testify to all this?'

'To all what? I wouldn't want to go into open court and say that I'd slept with one boyfriend while another was waiting for me in my father's cottage. That sort of thing doesn't do a girl's reputation any good. I could testify that they tied me up, but I didn't see them thumping Justin Dennison.'

Detective Chief Inspector Cowiesson sat back in his chair. He presented a good poker face but Alice was sure that he was suffering frustration. She thought that she had given him very little to get hold of. 'The name of your overnight friend?'

Alice looked at her brother. 'Do I have to drag him into it?'

'I think you'd better.'

'Paul Henson,' Alice said, making a show of reluctance. The constable wrote down the address and checked it.

'Describe his house to me.'

Alice blessed her own forethought. 'I don't see the relevance. Anyway, it's a flat.' She repeated, almost word for word, the description that Paul had given her.

'Miss Dunwoodie,' said the DCI, 'there were rather a lot of possessions at the cottage which I can only suppose to have been yours, more than would be explained by what you've just told us.'

Alice was ready for that one. 'I've often stayed there. Sometimes I've had a girlfriend with me. During the winter, when I know that my father won't be going there, I keep spare clothes and some makeup and things. That way, if I decide on impulse to go there, I have what I need.'

'You mean, if you decide to take a boyfriend there?' The DCIs nostrils were flared with distaste.

Ronald put his oar in quickly. 'My sister's morals are no concern of yours, Chief Inspector. They are not against the law.'

'I have to have the facts before I can decide whether they're relevant or not. And her morals might be a concern of mine. She has admitted taking a female friend with her. If they were entertaining men there for money, that might constitute keeping a brothel and—'

'You have no evidence for any such supposition,' Ronald said quickly. 'It is a scandalous suggestion.'

'We'll leave it for the moment,' Mr Cowiesson said. 'On another subject, Miss Dunwoodie, have you ever used one of the phone boxes on Queen's Avenue?'

So they had made the connection. Well, it was fairly obvious. And having pushed hard to put her off balance, the DCI was closing in. 'I expect so,' Alice said. 'Before I got my mobile phone, I used call boxes all over the town.'

'But not recently?'

'No, not recently.'

'Miss Dunwoodie, about a week ago some false reports were phoned to the police, to divert cars away from the area where the supermarket was being broken into. Did you make any of those calls?'

'Certainly not.'

'You're absolutely sure that voiceprints of none of those calls will match voiceprints of your voice?'

Alice had puzzled over that very point during her wakeful hours. She hoped, without much hope, that recordings of a voice over a rather poor phone line would not provide adequate voiceprints for a prosecution, and the innocent wording of the DCI's question combined with the careful lack of guile in his expression, worried her. However, she had decided to gamble. 'Quite certain,' she said.

Her brother had been listening passively but now he stirred in his chair. 'Mr Cowiesson,' he said, 'not for the first time, my sister has answered virtually the same question more than once. She has been very frank and open with you. If you are accusing her of something, you'd better caution her and we'll get it out in the open. Otherwise, I think I should take her home now. She's still rather shaken by her experiences.'

'Very shaken,' Alice said.

Detective Chief Inspector Cowiesson got to his feet. 'I shall want to speak to you again,' he said. 'We have finished for the moment.

Chapter Twelve

They walked out into cold sunshine. The freedom and bustle of the street seemed almost jolly after the repressive atmosphere of the police building, saturated as it had been over the years by hatred, fear and shattered hopes, but Alice's mind was going full tilt. She could have admitted making the calls but have denied any more criminal intent. A conviction for making nuisance calls to the police would not be a hanging matter and her denial at this stage might be made to look bad later. It had been worth a gamble. She pushed the question of voiceprints to the back of her mind. There were a dozen others competing for her attention.

'Would you take me out to Dad's cottage, please?' she asked.

'What for?'

'I want to collect some of my things and make sure that it's lockfast. I don't remember turning the thermostat down.'

'You won't be going back with another boyfriend for a day or two?'

Alice looked at him sharply. Until then, he had been a rather remote sibling, some years older than herself, moving in an entirely different ambit and with interests barely overlapping with her own. But now his snide question seemed both concerned and censorious. His concern might be gratifying in one way, but she had no intention of being censured by one whose own lifestyle would have left much to be desired by the more conventional observer.

She waited until they were back in the car. 'I'm telling you as my lawyer that what I said to that policeman was the truth. Now I'm telling you as my brother that it's none of your damn business, that I'm not going to take even implied criticism from somebody who I know for a fact has bedded at least four of my friends and smokes pot most weekends – and that, truthfully, I have never slept with Paul Henson. Nor with Justin Dennison yet. Soon, but not yet. And if those conflicting truths are too schizophrenic for you, well, you can't stop being my brother so you'd better give up being my lawyer.'

After a moment, he smiled ruefully. 'Accept my apology. I can wear two hats. I'm quite used to it. A lawyer's life consists largely of ensuring that his client gets every advantage that the law entitles him to, whether he believes his client or not. You see, the lawyer's belief is immaterial. He may be wrong. Truth is whatever a court can be persuaded to decide that it is. I'll believe both of you.' He started the car and pulled out into the street.

'Thank you, Ronnie.' She had not called him that for years. 'What's more important is, did I satisfy Mr Cowiesson?'

'You didn't satisfy me, but I know you better than he does. I think you've left him uncertain. Not that it matters. It's what he can prove that counts. You realize that the police will probably still be in possession of the cottage?'

'Let's take a look anyway. And I want to visit Dad and Justin, but I can do that by bus if you want to hurry back to your own dissipations.'

'I never dissipate on Sundays before the sun goes down.' From which, Alice gathered that they were now confidants in misbehaviour.

As Ronald had predicted, the cottage was being examined by two men in plain clothes. They prevented her from reclaiming her computer or the leftover items of clothing and makeup but they promised faithfully to turn down the thermostat and lock up the cottage when they had finished. Alice was satisfied. She was sufficiently computer-literate to be absolutely confident that she had not allowed into any part of her computer's memory any material that she would not wish the police to see.

She waited until the car had entered the trees again. 'Stop, a moment,' she said. 'I want a pee.'

'You could have gone in the cottage.'

'I don't suppose those detectives would have emptied the toilet for me.'

She pushed her way between the trees. For several minutes she was sure that her bag had been found and removed. In her haste and in the darkness, she would certainly have missed some of the money in her bag. If the police had it, they would find some of the supermarket money and, more easily proved, the money which, according to the message relayed by her brother, was counterfeit; and they would have no difficulty in proving that the bag was hers. Worse, her fingerprints were on the notes. The inferences to be drawn would be damning. Action was called for, worry could come later. She forced her way between the low branches from one furrow to the next and back again to the other side. At last she found the bag. She must almost have crawled over it a minute earlier, but its colour blended into the dead needles and it had found a hollow; in the dim recesses among the trees it was almost invisible. She breathed a deep sigh of relief.

She found her brother standing beside the car with a mobile phone in his hand. 'Well, look what I've found,' she said airily. She dropped her bag into the boot and began brushing off the dead needles.

Ronald made no comment beyond raising an eyebrow and emitting a sound which she could only think of as a snort. He tapped his phone. 'Dad's been granted bail,' he said. 'My partner fixed it. So . . . the Infirmary first?'

'Please.'

Ronald drove to the Infirmary – a modern building in off-white concrete. This had replaced a much-loved but inconvenient and unhygienic Victorian predecessor which had now been converted into a business centre. Alice retrieved her bag from the boot and slung it over her shoulder. 'Wait five minutes,' she suggested. 'I may be kicked straight out on my ear. If they let me see him, I don't know how long I'll be. I can walk home or take the bus. And thanks.'

She had arrived during a scheduled visiting hour, so the hospital was bustling. Evidently, Justin was not considered either a serious suspect or an endangered witness, because she found him in a corner of a six-bed ward without anyone to guard him or to listen in on his conversations. He greeted her as nearly with open arms as circumstances permitted, but his first enquiry was after Humph's well-being. The police, he said, were visiting him at irregular intervals to enquire whether his memory had improved but otherwise they were leaving him in peace. One cracked rib had been strapped up. Tests and X-rays had found no more serious damage and his bruises were hurting him less with every passing hour.

'They said that I could be discharged tomorrow or the next day, if I had somebody to look after me.'

'I dare say that something might be arranged,' said Alice.

She and Justin had nearly an hour to converse in whispers, tying the loose ends of their stories together and agreeing just how much of Justin's memory could be allowed to return. And if their whispering sometimes strayed from that strict agenda into an area more deliciously personal, that was only to be expected. When visiting hour ended and visitors were ushered outside, she kissed him gently on his bruised lips and set off on the walk home with a light step. Only a few tricky hurdles lay between herself and a rosy future.

Alice's father had been bailed and was back at the family home before she returned there. Lunch was taken in a constrained atmosphere. Mrs Dunwoodie chatted feverishly about the more innocuous news of the day while Alice and her father made disjointed replies. As soon as the meal was finished, Mr Dunwoodie again invited Alice into his study; but this time his manner was not at all ominous but more suggestive of a meeting of minds on an equal footing. They took the pair of easy chairs.

'It's time we had another talk,' Mr Dunwoodie said.

'True,' said Alice. 'Perhaps if we'd been more frank with each other last time, we wouldn't have been at cross-purposes last week. But you weren't to know,' she added kindly.

Her father looked at her with a trace of his former manner but he allowed his irritation to pass. 'No need to get uppity with me, my girl. We're each as bad as the other. I was hardly likely to tell my daughter that I was involved in a major counterfeiting operation. It was just unfortunate that we had separate things going and they ran counter to each other. That was a nice little caper of yours, by the way. Who planned it?'

'I did. And please don't say anything about me being my daddy's girl. All the same, I'm properly grateful to you for getting me off the hook as you did.'

Mr Dunwoodie shrugged. 'I didn't have a hope in hell anyway. Did it do the trick? Are you in the clear?'

'Given some luck and a lot of careful planning, the worst they should be able to pin on me would be making nuisance phone calls to the emergency services. That's assuming that none of my friends gets arrested and talks. But what about your men? Are any of them likely to come after me?'

'They know better than that.'

Alice hesitated and decided that it was better out in the open. 'Dad, is it going to be very bad for you?'

'Who knows? It's amazing what a good barrister can do with a few legal technicalities and a golden tongue. Whatever happens, it's happened before.'

'Has it?' Alice had always seen her father as a pillar of local society.

'Oh yes.' He produced the smile which had figured large in her childhood memories. 'There's no point trying to keep secrets from you now. Do you remember when you were four or five? Your mother explained that I was working abroad, Peru or somewhere. I did fifteen months out of a two-year sentence in Ireland for a "long firm" fraud. Under another name, fortunately, so I can still be passed off as a first offender.' Mr Dunwoodie ran his fingers through his grey but still thick hair. 'Alice, I'm sorry if I came over as the heavy father last time we talked, and I'm even sorrier if, in retrospect, I look like a hypocrite. But if you think back, you may remember that I never suggested that you should follow in my footsteps.

I wouldn't want you to do that. In a way, it's a pity – I could have used a trustworthy lieutenant who was unlikely to arouse suspicion. And, of course, if you'd come in with me we wouldn't have fouled things up for each other. But that's spilled milk. I want better for you. Find some nice young man and drag him to the altar.'

Alice resisted any temptation to refer to male chauvinist pigs. 'I have found a nice young man,' she said. 'Unfortunately, you found him first. Justin Dennison. Your engraver,' she reminded him when her father failed to react.

'Oh.' Mr Dunwoodie made a small gesture which might have been of apology. 'That was unfortunate. I ask you to believe that I never ordered any violence. It was important that we got the money back—'

'Because it was dud?'

'Mostly, yes. I told the men to recover it and they took matters into their own hands. He's going to be all right?'

'So he tells me.'

'And has he learned a lesson?'

'I don't think that either of us will stray off the straight and narrow again.' Alice hesitated. The habit of years was hardly to be broken overnight. 'I'll probably move in with him straight away,' she said bravely. 'Marriage can come later. Will Mum will be able to manage? Financially, I mean. And will she mind being alone? I shan't be very far away.'

'She won't be short of a pound or two, most of it quite legitimate. I wouldn't be much of a financial adviser if I couldn't give myself the best advice of all.'

'If you didn't need the money – do you mind my asking? – why did you step outside the law?'

'Ask away. But I don't know that I can give you a clear

172

answer. Sometimes life seemed to be just too damn boring. Can you understand that?'

Alice thought it over. 'Yes, I think I can.'

'There you are, then. Pitting your wits against opponents across the bridge table or in business is all very well. There's a special thrill in taking on the forces of the law, because there's a real risk of losing more than mere money, but you have to remember that you can't win every time. That's why I want you to stay clean. I won't read you any more moral lectures.'

'Well, thank you for that much,' Alice said.

Mrs Dunwoodie, when consulted, proved to have far more moral flexibility than Alice had ever given her credit for. If the worst came to the worst, she said, she would be happy to have the house to herself for a while and woe betide any intruder who thought that she would be an easy target. She was far more concerned that Alice should get a ring on her finger before giving any thought to the continuation of the human species.

So Alice phoned for a joiner to meet her at Justin's house to repair the damaged door. She then begged a ride there with a load of her more useful or precious possessions. Her mother came in with her and together they began the task of setting the house to rights. Temporary repairs to ripped upholstery were carried out with the use of Duck tape from the corner shop. The kitchen was given an overdue scrubbing. When the house was as far restored as they could manage, they set about Justin's clothes while they argued about possible colour schemes.

Mrs Dunwoodie was happy to be occupied but Alice was nest-building.

For rather more than a week, life had been hectic and

unfamiliar for Alice, demanding frequent revisions of her attitudes to life. Now the pace slowed. It was a bittersweet period but the highs outweighed the lows.

Justin's return, and his surprise at finding a house which was much more orderly than before the intruders had gone to work on it, was definitely a high. Alice was happily busy. Justin was still unfit for any physical activity, so she nursed him and waited on him, visited his workshop to collect any mail and answer any urgent enquiries and even managed some overdue tidying in his small garden. But all the while she was thinking ahead and on their first evening together she coached Justin in what he should say in the event of certain enquiries.

On only its second day, the idyll was interrupted by an invitation for Alice to visit Detective Chief Inspector Cowiesson again. She was left in no doubt that it was not an invitation which was open to refusal. She accepted a ride in a marked police car with a return of the fluttering in her stomach. This could be make-or-break time. Justin had tried to insist on coming with her but, quite apart from still being unfit to travel, his presence could have proved more of a hindrance than a help. Alice left him reclining fretfully on his couch with the day's papers and a good book.

Once again, she was kept waiting in the interview room. This, she guessed, was a part of the DCI's technique of giving the visitor time to recollect past sins and dread the coming interrogation, so she ran over her story once more in her mind and then thought about Justin.

DCI Cowiesson, when he deigned to arrive, was brisk. 'No solicitor, this time?' he commented.

Alice shook her head. 'I'll ask for him if I feel that I need him.'

'I hope this means that you're going to be frank with me.'

'If I can,' Alice said.

Mr Cowiesson looked at her sharply but made no comment. 'Tell me what you know about the raid on the supermarket,' he said abruptly.

'If I knew anything, I would tell you,' Alice said. 'But I don't.'

DCI Cowiesson moved on, but from his expression Alice was sure that the subject had not been dropped, only put to rest. 'Then tell me about the telephone calls to the police while the raid was going on.' When Alice hesitated, he went on, 'I may as well tell you that your voiceprint from the last statement you made has been compared with voiceprints from the recording of those phone calls. We have two experts who are prepared to swear that they match beyond any possible doubt.' He saw Alice glance from the accompanying constable's notebook to the tape recorder and produced one of his faint smiles. Alice thought fleetingly that another part of his technique was to convey an impression of reading a suspect's innermost thoughts, but that he was merely reading body language in the light of logical deduction. 'Yes,' he said, 'my statement is going into the record. You are in no danger of entrapment. I don't play that sort of game.'

'In that case,' said Alice, 'I may as well make a full and final statement. I did not know anything about any raid on a supermarket but I did make three phone calls. That evening, I went out with my boyfriend, Justin Dennison. We called at a pub. I don't know the name of it – he might remember. A man who was sitting alone at a next-door table got into conversation with us and bought a round of drinks. I can't remember how he worked the talk round to the subject of emergency phone calls, but it seemed quite logical at the time. We seemed to be laughing rather a lot. You see, Chief Inspector, I don't have a very good head for drinks and I have a suspicion, almost a certainty, that my drink had been spiked. Before I knew it, he'd bet me a hundred quid that I wouldn't make three phone calls and I'd taken him up on it. You see, a hundred pounds is a lot of dosh when you're as unemployed as I am, but the laugh seemed, at the time, just as important as the money.

'Justin was horrified. He told me that I'd be committing an offence and that I might even be preventing the police from getting to where somebody was being robbed or attacked. The mood I was in, I thought that he was a bit over the top but I decided to humour him. When I tried to back out of it, the man said that I'd lost my bet and I owed him a hundred.'

'He could hardly have sued you,' the DCI said.

'I thought of that later. At the time, it seemed compelling. Anyway, I don't welch on my debts but I didn't have a hundred to blow and Justin certainly wasn't going to give it to me. And, I told you, I'd had a few drinks which were ten times stronger than I'd expected. The upshot was that I made the calls in the form he'd told me to, but I kept them as short as I possibly could. I may as well tell you now that I never collected my winnings. While I was making the third call, the man vanished.'

'Describe the man.'

Alice had considered offering a description of Tod. It would have served him right for his scurvy treatment of her before the van left. But his had been the reaction of panic and she still retained a fading affection for him. Anyway, if Tod were to be apprehended in connection with the supermarket robbery it would reopen a can of worms which she was trying very hard to close. In the van's headlights she had had a fleeting glimpse of the man who had chased Sarah through the hotel. He had been one of the men who had beaten up Justin and, presumably as a result of Tod's use of the jack-handle, he had not been present to be arrested at the cottage. Alice described him as best she could. If by any chance the police recognized the description, let him deny complicity in the supermarket robbery. It would only be expected. If asked to pick him out of a line-up, she could plead uncertainty.

'How would he know that he would find a foolish girl to make his calls for him?'

'I don't suppose that he did. He was probably prepared to make the calls himself if he didn't find some fool like me.'

DCI Cowiesson looked her in the eye. 'You're asking us to believe that you made phone calls which distracted the police from a crime but had no knowledge of the crime itself?'

'That is exactly what I'm telling you. Next morning, I felt awful – realizing what I'd done but having the hangover of a lifetime, far worse than I'd have expected for all that I'd drunk. That's when I became sure that the man had spiked my drink. I knew that I couldn't be any help to you at all, except by describing that man. And this morning I decided to write down his description and send it to you anonymously, but it's too late now. Anyway, I've given it to you.'

'As you say, it's much too late to pretend that your frankness is spontaneous. Who made the other phone calls?'

Alice raised her eyebrows. 'Were there other phone calls? I didn't know that.'

The DCI leant forward and held Alice's eyes. 'Miss

Dunwoodie, I'm absolutely sure that you know more than you're telling us. You'd be well advised to tell us all about it.'

'I have told you all about it,' Alice said indignantly. She donned her most supercilious expression, the one that she had usually reserved for wood-be seducers or impertinent shop assistants. 'I can't help what you choose to believe or disbelieve, Chief Inspector. I have no control over your mind. I've told you what I know. If that isn't good enough for you, I want my solicitor present. And I'm not saying another word until he's here, and probably not then.'

DCI Cowiesson was not so easily deterred. The inquisition lasted for a further half-hour, apparently wandering off into a morass of trivia and suddenly returning to the robbery from a fresh direction, but Alice remained passively silent. She thought that he received a signal, because he suddenly said, 'Very well. I shall be charging you with making nuisance phone calls to the police. Other charges may follow. That's all for now.'

Alice left the building on trembling knees. She was not offered a ride back to Justin's house, but the distance was less than a mile. When she walked in, Justin was evidently unsettled. 'You must be psychic,' he said. 'There was a plain-clothes bobby at the door, asking me about the man and the phone calls. I told him exactly what you said to say. I said that I couldn't remember which pub it was but I gave him a vague description which could have been any one of several. And the same with the man. What do we do if they push it?'

'They won't,' Alice said. 'Not unless somebody drops my name, but Dad's sidekicks wouldn't dare, and if Tod or Foxy or Sarah get caught they'd know that I could do them more harm than good. I've already 'fessed up to making the calls so they don't need any more evidence about that. They'd have a hell of a job proving that I did have any connection with the robbery and they know it.'

'I only hope you're right,' Justin said.

Chapter Thirteen

In the beginning, Alice slept in Justin's spare bedroom. Chaste kisses were exchanged, but even a hug would have been too painful. The period of waiting was one of frustration but relieved by the slow escalation of intimacy.

In the course of a week, his cracked rib began to mend and his bruises faded. Alice became worried. Consciously or unconsciously, Justin seemed to have drawn a line which he was afraid or unwilling to cross. Alice tried to let him see that further advances across that line would be permitted or even welcomed, but Justin remained in the grip of irresolution.

A girl who had been reared in a less inhibiting regime might have said, 'Come on, your room or mine?' or might simply have taken things into her own hands . . . But Alice had frightened Justin off once before. Now, in her lonely bed, she thought and worried. She had managed to have a private word with Justin's doctor at the hospital, who, much amused, had declined to breach patient confidentiality but, as much by what he had declined to say, had conveyed to her that there had been no physical damage of that nature. The problem, therefore, was psychological. His first approach to her had been rebuffed. His second had resulted, indirectly, in a serious physical beating. That he should hesitate before renewing his approaches was understandable and, up to a point, forgivable. But only up to a point . . .

It was not a subject which she would have felt confident of discussing with him without causing offence. She decided, first, to try a different tack.

She borrowed a small pliers from Justin's workshop and, after beautifying herself with as much care as she had taken before their appointment at the Cameron Arms, she squeezed up the hook of her prettiest bra after engaging it and, without too much difficulty, contrived to put it on. With very little else under her dressing gown, she went to say goodnight to Justin.

'I can't get my bra unhooked,' she said. 'Would you mind?' Her dressing gown dropped to the floor and she sat down beside him on his bed.

It took Justin some seconds of fumbling to undo the hook. She felt his fingers shaking. She let the bra fall and turned towards him.

That was all that was required.

Alice was brought to court some weeks later. Ronald, representing her, managed to avert any possible connection with the supermarket robbery being dragged into the evidence. This meant that any suggestion that her drink had been spiked was also omitted, but Alice expressed regret for an impulsive act carried out on the spur of the moment and the influence of alcohol to which she was unaccustomed. She was given a small fine and a stern warning and bound over to keep the peace.

Her father, lacking any such extenuating circumstances, did not fare so well, but his counsel was able to argue that Mr Dunwoodie had not personally engraved the plates, made the paper or printed the notes. He was given three years and pronounced himself satisfied.

It was a local scandal but the backbiting soon died. Alice decided that the few former friends who now bypassed her were the sort of friends she could do without.

Mr Farquhar, the supermarket manager, received a stiffer sentence, as did the three men taken with Mr Dunwoodie. The other man, who had made contact with Foxy's jack-handle, was never suspected. Alice decided that the scales of Justice were sometimes a little lopsided.

For a whole year, Alice had heard nothing from Sarah, Foxy or Tod. Sarah's parents were naturally worried. Alice told them, in all honesty, that she had no idea where Sarah had vanished to; but when Mr and Mrs McLeod suddenly stopped badgering the police and the local papers for news of her and refrained from even mentioning her name, Alice guessed that Sarah had been in touch and had dropped at least a hint that publicity might be in nobody's interests.

Alice paid close attention to the media and, because her attention was focused by her personal interest, she picked out one strand from among the thousands of interwoven threads of crime. A small gang was making occasional raids, not always successfully, on business premises in various parts of Scotland. The gang, generally believed to consist of two men and a girl, seemed to be well versed in building construction and ingenious in its methods of circumventing security measures. They made one error, however, when the girl was caught on the security camera of a service station and featured on *Crimewatch*. Alice recognized Sarah despite the long black wig, vivid makeup and padding of the figure. In the background was somebody who could have been Foxy.

She was less certain of her identification when, after a gap of a year, Sarah walked back into her life.

Alice was still living with Justin. The redecoration of his house was almost finished and they had partially refurnished with the aid of his insurance company. Alice's supermarket money had bought them a top-of-the-range kitchen. They were supremely happy. Although they did not yet know it, another life was beginning to stir inside her, but a marriage was already planned for a month ahead and her father had been promised a compassionate leave from the open prison in order to attend it and give the bride away. Alice had taken over the business side of Justin's workshop, dealing with mail, orders, dispatches, accounts and VAT – the vital trivia which Justin had been inclined to neglect in favour of the more interesting art work. Alice had also coaxed the reserved Justin into mingling with what passed locally for café society, with the result that business was escalating. They had already engaged an assistant for the humdrum engraving of gifts and trophies, leaving Justin free to deal with the special clients who were beginning to beat a path to his door. Thanks to his engraving of a custom-built rifle which had then featured prominently in the sporting magazines, he was receiving frequent commissions, from the gun trade and private clients, for the engraving of lockplates and other parts of quality guns. His wildlife scenes were particularly admired.

Alice was getting out the monthly accounts. She was alone in the small office except for Humph, who was obliging enough to lick the envelopes for her, when a stout middle-aged lady entered the front shop. Alice leaned back to see through the door, looked twice and then again. Only the smile looked familiar and the restrained welcome which Humph gave the newcomer. 'Sarah?' she said uncertainly.

'Possibly,' said the visitor.

'Come through.' Alice studied her friend. Sarah was wearing what must have been a grey wig. Her makeup was also greyish except for a reddish tip to her nose and Alice had to look very close to see that a few wrinkles had been applied, very cleverly, with greasepaint. Severe clothes over body-padding, thick stockings and a large, leather handbag completed the picture. 'You're getting better at disguises,' Alice said. 'I recognized you on *Crimewatch.*'

Sarah looked alarmed. 'You didn't tell anybody, did you?'

'What do you think? You might have fooled me this time except that Humph doesn't usually stir himself for anybody who never gave him food. Sit down for a minute.'

Sarah subsided into the visitor's chair. 'Thanks. These shoes are killing me. They're supposed to be "sensible" shoes but I don't think that they're clever at all. I didn't want to chance putting you at risk by being seen here.'

'Good of you,' Alice said. She only had to swivel her chair to reach the kettle and switch it on.

'I'm like that, always thinking of others. You seem to have dug yourself a nice little burrow here.'

'It's pretty good,' Alice admitted. The kettle came back to the boil and while she made coffee she devoted a little time to telling her friend how satisfactory her life had become.

'You're never bored?'

'Contentment isn't boring,' Alice said. As she spoke, she wondered. 'Tell me about yourself. You're still with Tod and Foxy, aren't you?'

'Yes.'

'And are you and Foxy still . . . you know . . . ?'

'Both of them,' Sarah said smugly. 'Why make one person happy if you can make two? It's great. No jealousies. Sometimes we don't do it at all for weeks and then, after a job, it's three in a bed and honeymoon time. I've never had such fun. And the excitement of it! But we'll retire soon. The expenses are hellish, of course.'

'But no tax,' Alice said.

'There is that. Just equipment and bribes and having to live in hotels while we look for the next one. But we've done well. We've got a new van, by the way. Much more comfortable than the one you remember.'

'Bought it?'

'Well, no. Foxy drove it away from a showroom forecourt. But we've got almost enough put by to retire to Spain or the south of France. Just one more job should do it. Alice, there's this big jeweller's shop, not more than a hundred miles from here, full of stock and they do a lot of work on the premises so the safe's full of gems. We've even got a damn good offer to buy the lot from us.' Sarah opened her large handbag on the desk. 'I've got a plan of the building and the Ordnance Survey map of the street. The manager sleeps over the shop but he's away on Tuesday nights.'

Alice handed over a cup of coffee. 'But why are you telling me this?' she asked. 'I'm legit. I'm the honestest person you'll ever meet. I'm getting married in a few weeks.'

'I know, Alice, I know. But this one's tricky. What it needs is one of your clever plans with everything thought out and timed. If you're getting married, you can use a little capital. We thought twenty-five per cent, like before.' Sarah spread the Ordnance Survey map across the desk. 'You see, the back of the shop's overlooked from the back of this social club here. We need a distraction or some way to close the club for a night.'

Alice looked down at the Ordnance Survey. 'Perhaps just this once,' she said. 'Why not? Maybe I'd better come and look at it.'